He placed her palm on his bare shoulder

She wanted to move away, but she seemed rooted to the spot. Oliver moved closer, trapping her in his arms.

"What are you frightened of, Laurel?"

"I thought you were going to kiss me," she admitted huskily.

"So I was. Is that such a dreadful thing? It can be very enjoyable, if you'd just let yourself enjoy it. There's no sin in kissing someone, Laurel—look, I'll show you."

His lips moved gently over hers. Against her will her lips softened, and some of the rigidity left her body, but when Oliver's tongue stroked the outline of her passive mouth all her dormant fears awoke, and she sprang away from him.

"Why did you do that? You know I don't like it."

"You think you don't," he corrected. "As to why—call it atonement...."

HARLEQUIN PRESENTS
by Penny Jordan

These books may be available at your local bookseller.

For a free catalog listing all titles currently available,
send your name and address to:

Harlequin Reader Service
2504 West Southern Avenue, Tempe, AZ 85282
Canadian address: Stratford, Ontario N5A 6W2

PENNY JORDAN

savage atonement

Harlequin Books

TORONTO • NEW YORK • LONDON
AMSTERDAM • PARIS • SYDNEY • HAMBURG
STOCKHOLM • ATHENS • TOKYO • MILAN

Harlequin Presents first edition December 1983
ISBN 0-373-10650-5

Original hardcover edition published in 1983
by Mills & Boon Limited

CHAPTER ONE

LAUREL sighed as Sally, the office junior, popped her head round her office door for the umpteenth time that afternoon and enquired with breathless anticipation, 'Has he arrived yet?'

Barely glancing up from her typewriter, Laurel shook her head, 'And when he does, I won't be the first to know, Frances will, and Mr Marshall won't be too pleased if he finds you in my office again, Sally. You know he's in a hurry for that photocopying.'

'Oh, honestly, you haven't a romantic bone in your body!' Sally complained, ignoring Laurel's warning. 'Here we are, about to receive a visit from practically the most famous writer in the country, and all you can do is moan about old Marsh's photocopying! Aren't you even the tiniest bit excited?' she probed. 'I saw him on television the other night, on a chat show. He's gorgeous, don't you think so?'

'Mr Graves is simply a prospective client as far as I'm concerned,' Laurel replied repressively. 'I've neither read his books nor seen him.'

'Then you're missing a real treat on both counts,' Sally told her roundly, adding enthusiastically, 'Don't you think there's something smoulderingly sexy about dark-haired men——?' She broke off when she saw Laurel's face. Although Laurel had worked for Marshall and Marshall, Chartered Accountants, just as long as she had done herself, and in spite of all her questions, Sally knew little more about the older girl than she had done the first day she took over from Mary, Mr Marshall senior's secretary, who had retired.

She could be attractive, if only she would do something about herself, Sally decided judiciously. The single golden bar of sunshine striking across her desk revealed tinges of dark red in the tightly drawn back hair in its neat chignon. Laurel couldn't be more than twenty-one or two, but to judge by the way she dressed—in dowdy tweed suits and matronly blouses, her shoes sensible and sturdy rather than chosen to enhance the delicacy of her narrow bones—anyone would be forgiven for thinking she was a woman in her forties at least. She never wore make-up, and yet her skin had a translucent quality that Sally frankly envied. No one had ever heard her talk about her family, or indeed about anything unconnected with the office. Did she have a boy-friend? Remembering the way she always looked when the conversation turned towards boys and sex, somehow Sally doubted it. It was her considered opinion that for some reason Laurel had a hang-up about the opposite sex, but none of her probing had been able to reveal why. And yet she liked Laurel. She was the most senior secretary in the large accountancy firm, and yet by far the most approachable. She might drive herself to achieve almost impossible perfection in her work, and yet she always had time to help her, Sally, when the wretched photocopier started to spew out erratic copies; she was never above giving her a hand with the mail or with making the tea. Quite, different from Frances on reception who was supposed to help her.

At the thought of Frances Sally grimaced a little. Trust her to have all the luck! What Laurel had said was quite true; she would be the first one to see Jonathan Graves when he walked into the office, for his appointment with Mr Marshall, and no doubt she would make the most of it. Cat, Sally thought acidly, mentally comparing her own plumb brunette ordinariness with Frances' cool Nordic looks, to her own detriment.

'Are you honestly not even the slightest bit curious about him?' she questioned Laurel curiously.

A faint smile touched Laurel's mouth. Poor Sally, she was obviously finding it hard to believe that Laurel didn't share her interest in their latest client. Bitterness replaced her smile. None of the male sex held any interest for her; what she did feel for them was uninterest if they happened to be as dry and distant as Mr Marshall, or a combination of fear and loathing if they happened to show any personal interest in her. It was a reflex action so deeply ingrained in her now that she was unaware of it; unaware of how much she shrank from even the briefest contact.

The trainee accountants in the light, airy room they shared on the floor below often discussed her—something which would have horrified her had she known of it, but she had lived deeply embedded in her own shell for so many years now that she was unaware of their thoughts. The male sex was a completely alien race to her. There had been no men at the convent where she had been sent after . . . after she had found herself all alone in the world. Initially they had sent her to a home, but her nightmares, her refusal to make contact with the other teenagers there had resulted in her being removed and sent to the convent.

She had been happy there in a subdued way, had even contemplated taking the veil, but the

Reverend Mother had gently but firmly dissuaded her. She did not have enough experience of life to make such a decision, she had told Laurel, and there was no true vocation.

Of course, Laurel had known that was not the real reason she was being sent away; Reverend Mother was trying to be kind, to pretend that Laurel was not being rejected; but Laurel had known differently—and why!

Her fingers clenched over her typewriter keys, her sherry brown eyes darkening with remembered pain and horror. Her whole body started to tremble inwardly and she had to fight against the betraying sickness welling up inside her, the agonising memories she had sworn never to relive.

'Laurel, are you all right?'

Sally's anxious voice cut through her thoughts, banishing the threat of the past.

'I'm fine,' she lied, glancing at her watch. 'How about a cup of tea?'

Frightened by what she had seen in the normally calm sherry-coloured eyes, Sally willingly complied. For a moment it had been like looking at a complete stranger; a different Laurel who had known an anguish and horror too great for her to comprehend.

They drank their tea in silence—Laurel was like that, not given to chatter or confidences, and yet for all her unworldly appearance, her frumpishness, Sally was suddenly struck by the thought that nothing one could tell Laurel about the sins and omissions of the human race would truly shock her. Quite why she should think this Sally didn't know, and she tussled mentally with the problem for several minutes before realising that it was gone three o'clock and she would have missed Jonathan Graves' arrival in the foyer. This was confirmed when the intercom on Laurel's desk buzzed commandingly.

Laurel reached for it, and listened in silence for several seconds.

'Mr Marshall wants me to go in and take notes,' she told Sally, gathering up her notebook and two pencils. 'It could take some time, so I think you'd better make a tray of tea. I'll take it in with me.'

Marshall and Marshall was the old-fashioned type of firm that still believed in treating its clients in a courteous and leisurely fashion. Most of them were older people; and while Laurel didn't mind this, Sally made no secret of the fact that she would have preferred to work somewhere with a more modern image.

Having checked that all was in order on the tea-tray, Laurel paused briefly to examine her reflection in the mirror, checking for any hairs straying from her immaculate chignon. There were none. There never were. Once, when she was at secretarial college, some of the other girls had tried to persuade her to wear her hair down. They had even tried to wrest the pins from it. Laurel paled at the memory, her eyes huge in the delicate triangle of her face.

Her bone structure was as fine as a bird's. She was almost frighteningly slender, her skin very Celtically fair—an inheritance from the father she had never known.

He had been a Scot; a born wanderer, her mother had always said, and he had been killed in Hong-Kong during a riot there. Her mother hadn't seemed to mind and Laurel suspected the marriage had not been particularly happy, but as she couldn't remember him she felt no personal sense of loss. For as long as she could remember there had simply been herself, her mother and her grandparents: all living together in the large old house her grandfather had bought for his bride in Hampstead, within sight of the Heath. She had been happy in those days—happy and carefree. There had been a dog, a liver and white spaniel to yap at her heels and chase imaginary rabbits over the Heath. She had gone to a small local girls' school which she had loved.

But then first her grandmother and then her grandfather had died, and there had only been her mother and herself in the huge old house, and very little money for its upkeep. Which was why her mother had started taking in lodgers.

Her hands shook, rattling the cups on the tray. She must pull herself together. What was the matter with her? There was no going back—she knew that. She had a lot to be grateful for; her small flat in the quiet block inhabited in the main by older couples, her small car which she drove into the country whenever she could spare the time. Something about the timelessness of the country landscape, the rightness of nature's cycles had a beneficent effect upon her tensed nerves.

She was completely alone now. Her mother had always had a weak heart, and after ... after the trial she hadn't been able to endure the shame of what had happened and had slipped quietly away from life; away from her, Laurel acknowledged with self-condemnation. There had been a time when she thought that she ought to have been the one to die, not her mother, but that would have been too easy, too kind a fate. The gods had a different punishment for her.

She knocked and pushed open the office door. Mr Marshall as the senior partner in the firm had the largest office; one that, with its solid mahogany furniture, panelled walls and hunting scenes conveyed an air of solid respectability; no bad thing for a firm specialising in accountancy.

'Oh, Laurel, you brought us some tea, Excellent.'

Mr Marshall permitted himself a thin dry smile. Laurel was the best secretary he had ever had— quiet, self-effacing and yet unbelievably efficient. He had been doubtful at first when the head of the typing unit had suggested her as a replacement for Mary Gilmour, but it had taken less than a month for him to appreciate the excellence of her choice, and Laurel had been appointed as his secretary. He glanced at her now. Her woollen suit in a muted honey brown was efficient and neat; a pristine white blouse with a high neckline and a row of pintucks down the bodice effectively-concealed the shape of her body, as did her heavy skirt, but not even the thick tights and sensible shoes she was wearing could detract from the slender length of her legs, and as she poured the tea at her employer's command, Laurel was bitterly aware that the man seated opposite Mr Marshall, whose profile she couldn't see without lifting her head, which she firmly refused to do, was quite openly and appreciatively studying them.

'Leggy' was how her grandmother had been wont to describe her, and at five foot eight, Laurel did have a length of leg that smaller girls openly envied. Indignation flashed in her eyes as, out of the corner of her eye, she saw their new client bend towards the floor, supposedly to remove some papers form the briefcase he had placed there, but Laurel knew that she was the focus of his attention, and a dark, smouldering anger burned up inside her; her voice was icy with dislike as she asked him whether he preferred milk or lemon in his tea.

He lifted his head and turned towards her, and

Laurel felt the blood draining from her face, a low buzzing sound in her ears. It couldn't be . . . but it was . . . every single detail of that face was burned into her mind with acid; there was no way she could forget or mistake it.

From a distance she heard Mr Marshall saying her name testily, and from somewhere she found the strength of will to lift the cup and saucer, proffering it to the man who called himself Jonathan Graves, but whom she knew by the name of Oliver Savage. And he had recognised her. She had seen it momentarily in his eyes before he had concealed his shock. She was bitterly glad that he had been shocked; what had he expected, or had he simply dismissed her from his mind, after he had destroyed her and left her feeling that death would be a merciful release from the only alternative life now offered her.

'Sit down, Laurel,' Mr Marshall instructed her when she had passed him his tea. 'Mr Graves, or Mr Savage, as I believe he prefers to be called, would like to take away with him some brief notes on our discussion. Mr Savage, as you may know, is a writer,' he explained pedantically. 'He has been living and working abroad for some time, writing under the pen-name of Jonathan Graves, but he now intends to return to this country and is seeking advice as regards tax matters.'

Jonathan Graves and Oliver Savage, one and the same man; what sort of books did he write? Laurel's lips curled fastidiously. She could make a fair guess. They would be tainted with the same sort of sensationalism he had brought to his work as a journalist. Men like him shouldn't be allowed to write, to condition the minds of others with their skilfully manipulative lies. Truth to them was simply something to be twisted and warped until it was a broken unrecognisable thing, just as she. . . .

Only the superhuman strength of will that had carried her through the last six years enabled her to sit down and make notes of the discussion that ensued between her employer and Oliver Savage. Although she refused to betray it, she was aware of every nuance of his voice, every inflection behind the words. The sickness she had experienced on first seeing him so unexpectedly had faded, leaving in its place an anguished fear. What if he should try to talk to her, to. . . . But no, she couldn't bear that. All the time her pencil skimmed busily over the lined paper of her shorthand notebook her thoughts collided and entwined, writhing formlessly like snakes inside her head, confusing and bewildering her. She had deliberately angled her chair so that she wouldn't have to look at him, and it came as a shock, when she raised her head for a momentary respite, to discover that he had shifted his and that he was searching her face, as though he wanted to lay bare the bones beneath the skin and delve into the secret recesses of her mind. He had always instilled fear in her, but now her fear was greater. It gripped her, stifling her, tensing her body, leaving her face pale and her eyes strained.

It was a relief when Mr Marshall started speaking again and she was free to bend over the notebook, blotting out the image of his face. A sexy face, Sally had called it on more than one occasion, when trying to persuade her to study his dust jackets. She hadn't been interested enough to even glance at them—an omission she regretted now, because had she done so she would have been prepared for this meeting, would in fact have been able to avoid it. He moved, the long line of his thigh intruding on her vision. Sickness clawed at her stomach, and her fingers slackened over the pencil, so that it slid from them on to the floor.

They both bent to retrieve it together, and because his arm was the longer, expensively encased in dark suiting, a gleaming white shirt cuff circling the sinewy masculine wrist, he reached it first, his arm brushing against the exposed flesh of Laurel's for the merest fraction of a second—but it was long enough to have her cringing away from him, her eyes dark with terror and loathing, emotions which he registered with hooded grey eyes before handing her her pencil.

He had not changed, Laurel thought sickeningly, or if he had it was simply to become more intensely male, even more dominant and powerful. She had sensed the power in him right from the first; sensed and feared it, and because of what had gone before her rawly scraped nerves had responded badly to it, and because of that he had trapped her in the nightmare web of questions he had thrown at her. Questions which had eventually destroyed her and killed her mother, while he and. . . .

With an almost physical effort she wrenched her thoughts away from the past and back to the present. Why should he have changed, after all? Six years in the life of a man of twenty-seven were hardly likely to have the same cataclysmic effect as six years tacked on to the life of a girl of fifteen, for whom they represented a flowering and growing such as she would never experience again. Only Laurel had never experienced that flowering; it had withered and died. In six short months she had grown from a child to a woman, with a burden of knowledge she had found too heavy to carry. Mechanically she took down Mr Marshall's careful speech. Sally was always complaining that working for Marshall and Marshall was dull and boring, but Laurel didn't find it so. To her it represented security and safety, just as her old-fashioned clothes and primly repressive appearance did. Once, like Sally, she had delighted in pretty clothes and even tentative experimenting with make-up. But all her femininity had been frozen inside her and nothing could ever thaw it now.

She was glad when Mr Marshall signified that she could leave. There had been a look in Oliver Savage's eyes when he recognised her that she remembered; a questioning, searching look that said that he wouldn't simply leave matters where they stood. Perhaps he was no longer an investigative reporter; but he had obviously never lost the instinct of hounding people; of questioning and badgering them until they gave him what he wanted, just as she had done. . . . But he would never get the opportunity to question her again. He had destroyed her once, and the woman who had emerged from the ashes of that destruction was impervious to the Oliver Savages of this world.

'Goodness, you look pale—are you all right?' Sally questioned when she emerged into her own office. When Laurel nodded her head, she added in a more enthusiastic tone, 'Well, come on, tell me all about him. Is he as incredibly sexy close up as he is in his pictures?'

'I didn't look.'

Sally grimaced, obviously not surprised by the lie. And it was a lie, for she had looked, searching that all male face for some tinge of compassion or regret, but there had been none. Only arrogant maleness.

'I suppose they'll be in there hours yet,' Sally

protested, 'You know what old Marshall's like once he gets going. Have you got much to do?'

'Only these notes. They shouldn't take long. I'm leaving early tonight,' Laurel announced, averting her face so that Sally wouldn't guess how sudden this decision was. 'I'll leave the notes on my desk before I go, but I'm going to have to rush.'

'Okay, I get the message,' Sally told her, taking the hint and sliding off her desk. 'It's time I was rounding up the mail anyway.'

Once she had gone Laurel concentrated on typing back her shorthand, glad of the solitude of her office which offered no outside distractions. It took her just over an hour, and towards the end of it she was holding her breath as she raced to get the work finished before the meeting inside her boss's office came to a close. Some deep instinct was urging her to get away, to leave the office before Oliver Savage walked in and found her there. Savage by name and savage by nature, she thought numbly. And she had been savaged once by his merciless talent for destruction, she wasn't going to let it happen again.

She had just pulled the last sheet from her machine, and was reaching for the cover, when Sally suddenly burst in, her curls tangled, a smudge of ink on one cheek.

'Thank goodness you haven't gone!' she exclaimed. 'Laurel, it's the photocopier. The wretched thing just won't work, and John Lever wants a dozen copies of some document running off before I leave. He wants to send them out in tonight's post. . . .'

'I'll come and have a look at it.'

Laurel was halfway down the corridor before she remembered that she had left her handbag in her office and that she would have to go back for it. She hesitated, and Sally, suddenly impatient, grasped her arm, tugging her towards the general office. 'Come on,' she urged. 'He's going mad with me, you know what he's like'.

It took longer than Laurel had anticipated to find the problem—a piece of paper jammed inside the copier, but eventually she managed to get it working again, and at Sally's insistence remained at her side while it ran off a dozen perfect copies of the requisite document.

Her hand was on the door of her office when she heard voices inside, and she was just about to retreat when Mr Marshall opened it, his frown relaxing as he saw her.

'Ah, Laurel, I was just telling Oliver that it isn't like you to leave early. You've done the notes?'

Skirting her desk and carefully avoiding so much as glancing at the tall male figure standing by the window, Laurel proffered the typescript to her boss. Her handbag was by her desk, and she reached for it, her voice hesitant as she asked if she might leave.

Mr Marshall looked slightly surprised at such unusual behaviour on the part of his perfect secretary. The phone rang before he replied and Laurel answered it. It was Mrs Marshall, and her boss excused himself to Oliver Savage to take the call in his own office.

Hastily grabbing her handbag, Laurel made for the door, but inexplicably Oliver Savage was there before, her, blocking her exit.

'Laurel . . . it is you, isn't it?'

His eyes held her mesmerised, unable either to deny or accept his question.

'I want to talk to you. I'll drive you home.'

'No!'

The word jerked past her lips, her eyes dilating in her pale face.

The grey eyes narrowed, studying her slowly, missing nothing of her clothes or appearance. Like someone on the threshold of a nightmare Laurel saw his hand reach out to her, touching her face. She cringed back, seeing but not understanding the hardening of his mouth.

'You've got a smudge on your face. Ink.'

He turned his hand towards her, showing her the ink on his own fingers from the contact with her skin.

'It's the photocopier. I....' I must get out of here, her mind screamed wildly, but she managed to subdue the impulse to give way to her emotions. Emotions trapped and betrayed. She had learned that lesson by now, surely? She had learned that screaming and panic achieved nothing, and coldly incisive questioning and lies all.

'Laurel?'

The warmly tender way he said her name sickened her. He had said it like that before ... before.

'I must talk to you. . . .'

'No!'

It was a low animal cry of pain, regretted as soon as she had uttered it, and she saw from the sudden darkening of his eyes that Oliver Savage had registered it.

She heard the faint click as Mr Marshall replaced his receiver and came out to join them. Quickly picking up her bag, she hurried towards the door, and then to her horror she heard Oliver Savage drawling coolly, 'You'll excuse us if we rush off, Marshall, but I've promised to give your secretary a lift. It seems she has an important date this evening.'

Mr Marshall positively goggled, and if she had been in a mood to appreciate it, Laurel must have been struck with the humour of the situation. Mr Marshall was plainly not used to thinking that his secretary might have a life outside the firm that she was anxious to run home to every night. Instead, she stammered a bitter protest, stifled beneath the coolly measured tones of Oliver Savage's voice as he murmured something about getting in touch and studying the notes, and then, her arm in his imprisoning grip Laurel was forced to endure the disbelieving stares of the girls in reception as she was marched past them and out into the late autumn evening.

Once outside she tried to tug herself free, anger lending a faint colour to her otherwise pale face.

'Just what do you think you're doing?' she hissed angrily at her captor. 'I have no intention of going anywhere with you or saying anything to you. . . .'

'Well, at least that's an improvement on the ice-cold maiden I saw back in that office. It's a relief to know you're not entirely subhuman, Laurel.'

'Is it?' Her wrist was caught in his free hand, the intimate contact of his flesh against hers shocking her into silence. No man had touched her since . . . since. . . . She made a small whimper of protest in the back of her throat, her eyes giving away more than she knew.

'Don't touch me!' She got the words out between clenched teeth, surprised to see how white he had gone.

'You don't like being touched, do you, Laurel?' he asked with quiet emphasis, reading his answer in the sudden tightening of her features. 'My word! I've been looking for you for five years, do you know that?'

Her wooden expression seemed to defeat him and she felt a momentary flash of triumph that she had been able to reduce him to a loss of words; he who had always been so clever with words, made them do his bidding, made them destroy her life.

'Laurel, we must talk. . . .'

'I don't want to talk to you!'

Someone jostled them accidentally, and he released her momentarily. It was enough. Deftly twisting away from him, Laurel ran, mingling with the crowds, allowing herself to be swept away with them, her heart thudding like thunder as she waited for him to catch up with her.

A taxi slid to a halt in front of her and disgorged its passenger. Without hesitation, Laurel leapt in, giving the driver her address, and as they pulled away from the kerb she had a fleeting glimpse of Oliver Savage's angry and disbelieving face.

CHAPTER TWO

SHE couldn't eat, couldn't even drink the cup of tea she had made for herself, and she paced her small flat restlessly before coming to a decision. Like a sleepwalker she went into her bedroom and opened the wardrobe, lifting the cardboard box out of the bottom. They had given her this when her mother died. She had been at the convent then and Sister Theresa had wanted to burn them, but the social worker had murmured the magic words 'mental therapy' and she had been allowed to keep the box. She had looked at them again and again in those first few months, reading and re-reading until her head was full of the words.

Now she was going to look at them again.

Her hands shook as she lifted first the album and then the newspaper cuttings from the box. Yellowed and slightly faded now, they were all clipped together in date order. Drawing a shuddering breath, Laurel looked at the first one.

'Teenage girl accuses stepfather of attempted rape,' screamed the headline.

There was a blurred, grainy photograph of her at fifteen, her long russet hair windswept and untidy. Rachel Hartford, the social worker in charge of her case, was holding her hand. Poor Rachel, she had been as bitter about the outcome as Laurel herself and had given up her job.

Beneath the first cutting were others, gutter-press cuttings, with stories made up of the gleanings of whatever the reporters had been able to learn from their neighbours.

Then there was the court case. Laurel started to tremble as she remembered the ordeal, the cuttings disregarded on the floor. That should have been the worst she had to endure. Rachel had been disturbed when she learned who the defence counsel was, he had a formidable reputation and was extremely expensive. Neither of them had known where her stepfather found the money to afford such a lawyer—at least, not then; and Laurel had gone straight from his clever mauling almost literally into the arms of Oliver Savage, who had skilfully soothed and questioned her. So skilfully that she hadn't even realised that he was a reporter until his article appeared. And he didn't write for the gutter press; his articles carried weight, and what he had written about her was something she couldn't endure to contemplate even now.

For her own sake the social services had sent her to a children's home after the hearing; her mother was already seriously ill and unable to look after her.

She glanced at the small bundle of cuttings clasped in her hand, the past hovering over her like a dark shadow.

'Don't shut it away,' the psychiatrist who had seen her at the children's home had told her, 'talk about it—work it out of your system.'

But because she had always been over-sensitive, because of her self-loathing and hatred of everything that had happened, she had locked it all away, becoming withdrawn and repressed.

If only she had known who Jonathan Graves was—but she hadn't, and now it was too late to stop the memories crowding in on her, taking over her mind, forcing her to remember. . . .

She had been thirteen when her grandparents

died, just on the threshold of womanhood. She had missed them dreadfully. To supplement the family income her mother had decided to take in lodgers; the big house near the Heath was too large and expensive for the two of them, and yet both were loath to leave it.

Their first lodger had been a teacher. Laurel had liked her. She taught at a large comprehensive school and Laurel had listened wide-eyed to her stories about it, comparing it with the small convent school she attended.

Miss Sayers had got another job and had left, and for a while Laurel had watched her mother's face grow pinched and worried. But then one day she had returned home from school to find her mother smiling at a strange man sitting on the kitchen table, drinking a cup of tea.

Laurel had disliked him on sight and had shrunk away when her mother introduced him as their new lodger.

He was some sort of salesman and seemed to work odd hours, because whenever Laurel returned home from school she invariably found him in the kitchen with her mother. This had always been their special shared part of the day, on which even her grandparents did not intrude, and Laurel had resented his presence. She disliked him altogether. He was only an inch or so taller than her mother, but powerfully built, and slightly balding. Laurel didn't like the way he watched her mother, or the way his eyes rested on her sometimes, as though he was aware of the feminine budding of her body beneath her school uniform. Always acutely sensitive, her defence system sprang into action whenever he was in the vicinity, the tiny hairs on her body prickling with dislike.

She longed to tell her mother how she felt, but

somehow a gulf had sprung up between them. Her mother seemed to like Bill Trenchard. Her cheeks and eyes glowed whenever she was talking to him, and one afternoon when Laurel came home from school a little early, as she walked into the kitchen they seemed to spring apart, guilt written large in her mother's eyes, satisfaction in Bill Trenchard's.

His air of satisfaction made Laurel feel sick. He had been kissing her mother; she sensed it with all the outraged instinct of her own growing sexuality.

She was just beginning to learn about sex at school from her friends; Laurel had always been slow to make friends and had no 'best friend' in whom she could confide her growing dislike of their lodger. All she could do was to acknowledge in her own mind that to think of her pretty mother and 'that man'—as she mentally thought of him—doing those things she had heard about at school made her feel physically ill.

She hadn't known then that it was a normal part of growing up to feel a certain amount of disbelief and revulsion towards the sexual act on first learning about it, and she had remained locked in a world of misery, hating herself for loathing a man her mother so obviously liked and yet unable to do a thing about it.

At night she prayed fervently that he would be transferred elsewhere, that he would leave; and then, as though to punish her, her mother announced that she and Bill Trenchard were to marry.

'Please understand, darling,' she appealed, seeing the disbelief and dismay in Laurel's eyes. 'I've been alone so long, and Bill is such fun. We'll be like a real family,' she promised. 'Bill adores you.... I know it will seem strange at first, because you've never had a father....'

'Bill isn't my father,' Laurel said bitterly, just as the door opened and he walked in.

For a moment she thought he was going to strike her, he looked so furious, and she cringed back instinctively, hoping against hope that her mother would change her mind.

As she shot out of the kitchen she heard Bill Trenchard comforting her mother. 'Don't worry about it, she'll come round. You know what they're like at that age. She probably fancied me herself. . . .'

Fancied him! Alone in her bedroom, Laurel shuddered with loathing, hot tears of misery sliding down her cheeks. How could her mother marry a man like that? How could she bear the thought of him touching her, of . . .? Like a nervous colt her mind skittered away. Bill was not a particularly fastidious man. She had seen him coming from the bathroom, draped merely in a towel. His torso was thickset and covered in coarse dark hair, as were his back and arms. The sight of his partially naked body revolted her, and she couldn't understand how her mother could endure to look at it, never mind touch it.

They were married within the month—a quiet register office ceremony. Laurel had had a new outfit for the occasion. Her mother and Bill had taken her shopping. She had hated it. Bill had chosen her dress, a brief mini which exposed the fine length of her legs. It was far shorter than anything she had worn before, and she had felt acutely selfconscious in it. She had worn her hair down; and it was only later, looking at the photographs with the eyes of an adult, that she had realised how provocative she had looked; the tight, short dress with its scooped neckline; her hair, long and thickly unruly, but at thirteen she hadn't been aware of such things and she had merely known that her new stepfather was looking at her in a way she didn't like.

After the ceremony Bill had taken them all out for a meal. They had had wine, and Laurel had a vivid memory of her mother looking flushed and happy. If only she could have stayed like that!

They weren't going away on honeymoon, but her mother had arranged for Laurel to spend the night with one of their neighbours. When she came downstairs with her case, after their return to the house, Laurel was surprised to find her stepfather alone in the kitchen.

'Your mother's just gone upstairs,' Bill informed her. His face was darkly flushed and when he came near her Laurel could smell the wine on his breath, sour and unpleasant.

'Well, now that you're my little girl, how about a kiss for your new dad?'

Laurel froze and stared uncomprehendingly up at him. She had kissed her grandparents, of course, and her mother, but some deep protective instinct warned her that kissing them was different from kissing Bill Trenchard.

'Still sulking, are we?' Bill demanded aggressively when she remained mute. 'Well, don't think I don't know why! Wishing you were getting a little of what's in store for your ma, is that it?'

Not really understanding what he was saying, but knowing that she didn't like the tone of his voice, nor the look in his eyes, Laurel started to move away, but Bill moved faster, trapping her against the sink.

'No need to get jealous, there's plenty to go round,' he told her thickly. His hands were large and sprinkled with dark hairs, and Laurel shuddered as they closed on her shoulders, his breath hot and sour against her face.

'Now. . . .' He was breathing heavily, as he brought his face down to hers. 'How about a kiss for your new dad?'

Laurel longed to scream, but she was too frightened. If only her mother would return! She hated the way Bill was touching her; the red moistness of his mouth. If it touched her own she would be sick, she knew it.

She heard her mother outside, and shook with relief as Bill released her, grabbing her case and rushing out of the room before her mother could see her fear.

All that night she barely slept. How could her mother marry a man like that? She longed for someone to confide in; someone to talk to, and she bitterly regretted the death of her grandparents. Slow painful tears coursed down her cheeks as she contemplated her future.

Some instinct made her say nothing at school about her hatred of her new stepfather, or the unwanted intimacies he forced upon her. Sometimes it was nothing more than touching her skin, other times it was worse, disguised as 'fooling about' so that her mother looked on fondly, while she was forced endure his hand on her body as he 'tickled' her—but at least he had never tried to repeat that horrid kiss.

Laurel thought he was doing it to punish her because she wouldn't accept him as her father, and to placate him and stop him from continuing to touch her she started to call him 'Dad'. But it didn't seem to have any effect, and she was always glad when his job took him away—sometimes for days at a time.

Then he lost his job. He had been married to her

mother for six months when it happened, and she seemed to grow pale and worried overnight.

There wasn't enough money now for her to stay on at the convent school, she explained gently at half term, and when school re-started Laurel would be attending the local girls' school.

It was ten times larger than her small private school and she felt lost in the huge classes and anonymity of the place. They were on a different syllabus and she was completely out of step. To make matters worse, Bill had started drinking, and she frequently heard him shouting at her mother and her mother crying.

One afternoon she came home from school to find Bill slumped in front of the television and her mother in bed.

'Sulking because she doesn't want me to go out tonight,' Bill pronounced, slurring his words the way he always did when he'd been drinking. 'Perhaps if she was a bit more fun to be with I wouldn't need to go out. Two of a kind, aren't you, you and your mother; neither of you know how to give a man a good time. Perhaps I ought to do some man a favour and teach you before it's too late.'

Laurel fled, seeking sanctuary in her mother's room. Her mother looked pale and tired, and Laurel couldn't bring herself to add to her worries by telling her what Bill had said.

Going to the larger school had opened her eyes a little, and she knew now that Bill shouldn't talk to her or touch her in the way that he did, but she knew that to complain to her mother would bring Bill's wrath down on her head. Her mother was too loyal to complain, but Laurel knew that she wasn't happy.

She had learned to become adroit about keeping

out of Bill's way. Unknown to anyone else she had bought and fixed a simple bolt to her bedroom door.

She knew from listening to the giggled confidences of the other girls about their boy-friends that there was more to sex than the basic animal coupling she had first thought, but remembering the revulsion she felt whenever Bill touched her she couldn't understand how anyone was able to enjoy it.

As far as Laurel was able to see, Bill was making no attempt to find another job, and they were all three having to live off the small capital her mother had been left by her parents.

Bill's drinking had increased too, coupled with a violence which could manifest itself in broken crockery and on one occasion a livid bruise to Laurel's arm when she had been too slow to obey his command for a second cup of tea. Increasingly Laurel was finding her mother in bed when she got home from school, her eyes strained and her face pale, but she never allowed Laurel to speak a word against her husband.

Laurel's fourteenth birthday came and went. Her mother suggested a small party at home, but Laurel had no desire for the other girls at school to be exposed to her stepfather. Unknown to herself she was drifting apart from her peers into a world of her own, where her stepfather stalked through her nightmares, and she went to school listless and drained.

It was the games mistress who noticed the bruise on her arm, and who questioned her about it. The school was a large one and Laurel wouldn't be the first case they had had of child abuse. Mrs Kellaway had trained at a large Northern school where she had learned quickly to see the telltale signs of beatings.

'I . . . I banged it on a door,' Laurel told her quickly, unable to prevent the deep flush staining her skin. 'It doesn't hurt.'

As Mrs Kellaway confided in the headmistress a little later, it could quite easily have been an accident, and Laurel was beyond the age for child battering.

'On the other hand,' she added, 'she's too withdrawn; living in a world of her own half the time. It might be as well to pay a visit to her home.'

The headmistress sighed and agreed. Mrs Kellaway was something of a new broom, and middle-class parents were apt to be vociferous in their complaints about teachers' interference in their pupils' private lives.

There was a week to go before the start of the summer holidays. Laurel had been studying hard for her exams, hating the thundery, stifling atmosphere pervading the Heath. The heat seemed to sap her strength, leaving her drained and tired, and she longed for a proper thunderstorm to clear the air. Her school books weighed heavily on her arm, and the closer she got to home the more her footsteps lagged. There had been a brooding menace about Bill these last few days that sharpened her fear; a look in his eyes that flooded her with an instinctive knowledge she fought against accepting. He wanted her physically. She could see it in his eyes, read it in his touch, and she shrank from the knowledge, deliberately keeping out of his way.

The kitchen was empty when she got home, and she heaved a sigh of relief at crossing this first hurdle safely. Sometimes he was there waiting for her, drunk and truculent, pinning her against the wall while he criticised her mother, his eyes roaming hotly over her body as though he could see the slender feminine shape beneath the school uniform.

She tiptoed past the living room, but it was so quiet she risked a glance inside. There was no sign of him. Perhaps he was out?

Her spirits lifting, she hurried upstairs. Her mother was in bed. She seemed to be shrinking daily, and Laurel had pleaded with her to send for a doctor. She had refused, and since she had no friends in the neighbourhood who called, Laurel had no one in whom to confide her fears concerning her mother.

'Bill's gone out,' her mother told her, in answer to Laurel's question, but Laurel noticed that she avoided her eyes, as though she too knew of her daughter's fear and the reason for it.

'How was school?'

Obediently, Laurel told her about her day, suggesting that she shower and then bring her mother a tray of tea. 'We could share it,' she suggested eagerly, 'just like we used to before. . . .' She bit her lip, knowing her mother allowed no criticism of Bill, but for once there was no soft reprimand from the bloodless lips.

'A tray of tea would be lovely,' was all her mother said.

A modern shower had been installed in the bathroom, at Bill's insistence, and during the work the old lock had come loose from the door. Bill had promised to fit it, but Laurel noticed as she walked into the bathroom that it had come free altogether. Closing the door, she stripped off and stepped into the shower, closing the curtain.

These last few months her body had changed dramatically. She was tall and slender with small high breasts and a narrow waist and hips. Her legs were long, tapering to fine ankles, her body almost that of a woman.

She showered quickly, enjoying the cool spray of the water on her heated skin. She was just showering off the last of the soap when the bathroom door opened.

'Well, well!'

She stood transfixed as her stepfather's eyes searched greedily over her body. He closed the door softly behind him and leaned against it. He had been drinking, Laurel could tell. She reached hurriedly for a towel, but he snatched it away, slurring this words as he said slowly, 'Not wanting to hide yourself away from your dear old dad, are you, Laurel? You know, the trouble with you, my girl, you're too repressed, frigid, like that mother of yours. . . .'

'You're not my father!'

Laurel said the first words that came into her head, her stomach crawling with sickness and shame for the way he was looking at her body. It was like the worst of her nightmares, when she was exposed and ridiculed, and she shrank back in horror as Bill reached out a hand and touched her still damp skin. A shudder rippled over her, and too late she saw the rage burning in his eyes.

'Think yourself too good for me, do you? Just like that mother of yours! Well, we'll soon see about that. You won't be so proud when I'm pleasuring that body of yours, my girl, you'll soon see. . . .'

'Get away from me!'

'Oh, come on, now, don't give me that innocent act. I know all about you girls. You're dying to know what it's all about really, aren't you? I've seen the way you look at me. . . .'

'Like I hate you!' Laurel spat at him, screaming

instinctively as he grasped hold of her naked body and lifted her out of the shower, his face livid and mottled as he bent over her.

'I'm your father, my girl,' he told her furiously, 'and you have to do everything I tell you. In my day a father took a strap to his kids if they didn't obey him. Is that what you want, Laurel?'

Still grasping her arm with one hand, his free hand went to his belt, and Laurel knew with sick certainty that he wanted to beat her nearly as much as he wanted her body. Her thoughts ran in terrified circles, her body tensing against him.

'Come on, you want it as much as I do. I've seen the way you look at me. I'm all man, Laurel,' he told her slowly, his eyes glittering with feverish excitement, 'and I'm going to prove it to you. . . .'

She screamed as his fingers kneaded her breast, his mouth hotly sour on her skin, and kept on screaming even when he shook her like a rag doll, almost throwing her to the floor in his rage.

'Don't make me angry, Laurel,' he warned her as he flung himself down on top of her. 'You've teased and tormented me enough, and I'm going to have you!'

Her body felt heavy and lethargic, crushed by the oppressive weight of his, but some instinct for survival lent her the strength to scream once more, the sound stilled by the sudden pressure of his mouth, making her gag sickly. He was going to rape her and there was nothing she could do to stop him. Tears ran from her eyes, terror making it impossible for her to move, and then outside the bathroom door she heard her mother's voice calling to her, saw her turning the door handle; saw the look on her face as she looked down on Laurel's sprawled naked body pinned to the floor by the heavy weight of Bill's.

Like a surly bear Bill clambered to his feet, but Laurel couldn't move. She felt frozen with fear and self-shame. She had seen the look in her mother's eyes as she stood in the doorway; a look that said quite plainly that whatever had happened Laurel was to blame.

'She drove me to it, Elaine,' she heard Bill mutter defensively, 'Always parading about in front of me with next to nothing on—oh, she's always careful to make sure she doesn't do it when you're around, but she's always been jealous— always wanted me herself. You know what teenage girls are like ... sex-mad, the lot of them. I couldn't help myself ... she was begging for it. ...'

Laurel wanted to deny his accusations, to plead with her mother for understanding, but somehow the words would not come. She knew she had not encouraged Bill—she loathed him, neither had she flaunted herself in front of him, but her pride would not allow her to beg her mother to believe her.

As Bill followed her mother out of the bathroom, he turned once, giving Laurel a look that warned her that it wasn't over, not by a long, long way.

Even with the lock on her bedroom door she refused to sleep that night, starting at every sound. She dressed for school in the privacy of her room, leaving early so that she could use the showers there instead of washing at home. Her body was bruised where Bill had touched her, and the sight of the finger marks against her breast made her retch dryly in shivering horror.

She found it hard to concentrate on her lessons. The last two of the day were gym. Half way though them the headmistress arrived, accompanied by a man—a school inspector, Laurel had later learned, but at the time all she had known was that he was a man and that for some reason he wanted to see her vaulting over the 'horse'. The mere fact that someone was watching her was enough to destroy her shaky confidence. She mistimed her leap and half fell over the horse, and might have injured herself quite badly if he hadn't leaped forward to catch her. But all she was aware of as his hands grasped her was that this was how Bill had held her last night, forcing her to the floor, touching her intimately, and as the world swirled and darkened around her, she was dimly aware of herself screaming, no, no, don't touch me!

When she came round she was in the headmistress's office. Miss Kellaway was there, but there was no sign of the man. Matron was also there and another young woman whom the headmistress introduced as Rachel from the Social Services Department, the significance of which didn't dawn on her until much later.

'Now, Laurel,' the headmistress began kindly, 'don't be frightened. We're here to help you, you know, my dear. . . .' She paused, coughed and looked a little embarrassed.

'Laurel, Miss Kellaway tells me that some time ago you came to school with a bad bruise on your arm. And now today, when you fainted . . . your body is very badly bruised, my dear, and. . . .'

The social worker interrupted gently, 'What Miss Laker is trying to say, Laurel, is that we believe you may have been sexually abused. . . . Yes, I know you don't want to talk about it, don't want to admit it even to yourself, but you aren't the first girl it's happened to, Laurel, and you won't be the last. We only want to help you, and there's nothing to be frightened of. You do know, don't you, that it's illegal for someone to have sexual relations with a girl under sixteen? And it's silly to get involved with such a rough boy-friend. Have you got a boy-friend, Laurel?'

She managed to shake her head, her whole body burning with the shame of what was happening to her. How could they understand? How could they know how she felt; how guilty and tainted; how much she hated her body?

'Matron will have to examine you, Laurel,' Rachel, the social worker, was saying in a soothing voice. 'Nothing to be afraid of. If you'll just go with her now. . . .'

Like a limp rag doll, Laurel went with her. The examination was painful and to Laurel humiliating, although she knew that Matron was deliberately trying not to hurt her, but afterwards she was sick, and she was still shivering when she was taken back to the headmistress's study.

'Matron tells us that you're still a virgin, Laurel,' Rachel announced, 'But I don't believe that you were a willing participant in whatever happened to you. We want to help you, dear. Why don't you tell us about it?'

She wanted to, but Bill had warned her that if she told anyone they wouldn't believe her.

As though she knew what she was thinking Rachel said softly, 'You have a stepfather, Laurel—was it him?'

She started to cry then and Rachel had comforted her, gently drawing the whole story out of her.

'Now listen to me, Laurel,' she said when she had finished. 'You are in no way to blame, in no way at all. You mustn't think that.' Over Laurel's head her eyes met Miss Kellaway's. 'Men like him ought to be shot,' she said bitterly. 'When I think of the damage he might have done. . .!

'Now, Laurel,' she said quietly, 'for your own sake it might be better if you lived away from home for a while. Not for punishment,' she added quickly, 'but to protect you.'

'My mother. . . .'

'Don't worry, we'll explain everything to her.'

Laurel hadn't argued, thankfully believing that her ordeal was over, but it was only just beginning.

CHAPTER THREE

THE Social Services Department installed Laurel with foster-parents; the start of the summer holidays meant that she didn't have to endure the curious questions of her classmates, and Miss Kellaway visited her regularly.

The only person who didn't visit her was her mother, and when Laurel asked repeatedly why, Rachel explained that she wasn't well.

'Try to understand, Laurel,' she explained. 'Your mother feels unbearably guilty because she exposed you to Bill Trenchard, and because she can't face up to that guilt she had shifted it on to you. In her eyes you're the guilty one, even though in her heart she knows that isn't true.'

'You mean she doesn't want to see me?'

Rachel sighed. This was one of the most heartbreaking cases she had had to deal with, and she longed to be able to do something concrete to help Laurel. The poor child's life lay in ruins around her, while the man responsible.... Her mouth tightened and she took hold of Laurel firmly, noticing as she did so how the thin shoulders flinched. Later on Laurel might benefit from talking to their child psychiatrist, but for the moment the scars were too new, too raw.

'Try to understand, Laurel, your mother has always been weak, has always needed someone to lean on.'

It was true, Laurel acknowledged, but she needed someone to lean on too. It came to her then that the only person anyone could safely rely on was themselves; that it was foolish to place any trust or reliance in another human being.

'We intend to prosecute Bill Trenchard,' Rachel informed her. 'He's guilty of sexually molesting a minor, and he must be punished for that, Laurel. You understand that, don't you?' Because if you don't help us some other girl will suffer—perhaps worse.'

Rachel meant that she still had her virginity, but her entire body and soul felt scorched, all emotion and feeling burned out of them.

'Would I have to tell people what happened?'

'Yes, but it will be worth it, Laurel, I promise you that.' And because she liked and respected Rachel Laurel believed her; believed that for the sake of some unknown girl Bill had yet to meet she had to see that justice was done. In those days she had still been naïve enough to believe that the truth must always be believed and respected, and even though her soul cringed from the thought of having to tell anyone about what had happened, because she knew not to do so was taking the cowardly way out, Laurel agreed.

It got into the papers—how, she didn't know, and although her foster-parents wanted to keep the articles away from her Rachel and the lawyer she brought to see her insisted that she must read them.

'Your stepfather obviously intends to claim that you led him on,' the lawyer explained to her, 'and I have to ask you, Laurel, did you?'

The look of sick revulsion in her eyes convinced him.

'I hate these cases,' he told Rachel later. 'And I've heard the stepfather intends to use Rowland Blandish. He's red-hot on defences for this type of case. I doubt if he'll get him off, but he'll really put her through it. I'll try to prepare her as much as I can. . . .'

'But he's guilty,' Rachel protested, 'and he might have destroyed her as a woman for ever. If you could have seen the look on her face when the school inspector touched her!'

'She's a sensitive child, which will make it ten times worse for her, and I agree with you, he's got to be brought to justice, but it's the mother I'm worried about. I tried to see her, but apparently she's confined to bed with a heart condition.'

'She refuses to see or communicate with Laurel, but then that's quite usual. In these cases the mother normally knows quite well what's going on and chooses to ignore it, but of course we aren't talking about incest here, we're talking about attempted rape.'

'Far harder to prove,' he warned her. 'And the courts and the public are hardening their hearts more and more against the victims; there's been too much press coverage on the subject; too many "claims" that have proved to be lies.'

'But in Laurel's case. . . .'

'Rowland Blandish will try to persuade the jury that Laurel led Trenchard on. She's a very attractive girl, Rachel, and whether we like it or not there are men who are always eager to convince themselves that teenage girls are eager for sex. You know that.'

'Yes,' Rachel agreed soberly, 'but Laurel isn't like that. I'm frightened for her.'

Mercifully Laurel knew none of this. She had withdrawn completely into her shell, unbearably hurt by her mother's defection and plagued by self-hatred. Had she in some way encouraged her stepfather? If she had she didn't know about it, but she had developed a fierce dislike of her body, to the extent that she would only wash in a darkened room. Despite the heat of summer she refused to dress in anything but thick sweatshirts and baggy jeans.

Mrs Lee, her foster-mother, reported this to the social services. A psychiatrist came to talk to Laurel, but she refused to respond.

The day of the court hearing arrived. The court was packed with reporters, and as her lawyer had predicted, the defence counsel tore her to shreds. Several times she broke down in tears, muddling her story, looking helplessly at Rachel, who could only listen with black murder in her heart, as she witnessed what was happening.

On the second day of the trial Rowland Blandish insisted that Laurel was to be dressed in teenage fashion clothes rather than her enveloping jeans and sweatshirt. He even produced an outfit for her. She put it on as the judge had instructed in a small room at the rear of the court.

It was a pink and white striped mini-skirt and a matching tee-shirt. The tee-shirt pulled tautly against the thrust of her breasts, the skirt showing off her long legs. Rachel bit her lip when she saw her. The judge had also instructed that she was to wear her hair down, and this she did. A glance in the mirror before she was escorted from the room showed her a stranger; a tall, slender girl with a mass of dark red-brown hair and a curvaceous figure.

She disliked the defence counsel's smile as she re-took the stand. 'Look at her,' he instructed the jury. 'Add make-up and the provocative manner of teenagers the world over and can any man be blamed for losing his temper a little, which is what happened to my client. As he is not her natural father isn't it also only natural that mingled with his anger should be desire? A desire any man might naturally feel. . . .'

And so it went on, question upon question, innuendo upon innuendo, until Laurel was ready to believe herself that she had encouraged him; that she was to blame.

The jury gave a verdict of guilty but with provocation, and Laurel left the court feeling besmirched and tainted.

The papers were flooded with articles on raising or lowering the age of consent for sexual relations; on the provocation of teenage girls in general, on rape and its side effects on the victims, and through it all Laurel remained silent and withdrawn.

The court had ordered that for own sake she was to be taken into care, which had resulted in her being sent to a home several miles away.

All through the court hearing she had heard nothing from her mother, and one afternoon when she could endure it no longer she left the school grounds and caught a bus for Hampstead.

She found her mother alone, lying in bed, looking tireder and older. Her face paled when she saw Laurel and she turned away.

'How could you come back here after what you've done?' she gasped. 'Shaming me, telling all those lies!'

'But Mother,' Laurel's mouth was dry. Her mother had seen with her own eyes, 'you saw. . . .'

'Your stepfather is right,' her mother said weakly. 'You're a wanton, Laurel. It's your father's blood coming out in you. No decent girl would dream of doing a thing like that! From now on you aren't my daughter.' She moved the bedclothes and Laurel saw the newspaper cuttings.

Sickness welled up inside her. Her mother was right: she wasn't fit to live. She ran out of the house, not seeing the car parked by the kerb, nor the man lounging against it, and ran full tilt into the road, oblivious to the blare of the horn of the oncoming car.

Strong arms grasped her, snatching her back from death. Furious, she pounded angry fists against the broad shoulders, gasping for breath when she was suddenly set free.

'You could have been killed!'

I wanted to be! The words trembled on the tip of her tongue, but remained unuttered.

'What's wrong?'

The man glanced from her to the house, and then frowned. He was taller, much taller than Bill, with a dark thatch of hair, tousled by the breeze. He was wearing jeans and an open-necked shirt. Dark hair curled at the base of his throat, and sickeningly Laurel remembered Bill's body; Bill's hands. She swayed and he caught her.

'Please. . . .' She shuddered as she pushed at his restraining hands. His eyes were grey and curiously blank, and yet she had the feeling that he was studying her minutely; the faded, baggy sweatshirt, the jeans, her hair tied back in a ponytail, her too fragile body and shadowed eyes.

'Live round here, do you?' he asked, releasing her and shifting his weight so that he was leaning against the car—a small powerful sports car, Laurel realised now.

'No!' The denial was quick and instinctive, but the raised eye brows insisted on some explanation.

'I was just visiting someone.' Unknowingly her eyes clouded 'Now I'm going . . . home.'

'Can I give you a lift?'

Strangely she knew she had nothing to fear from

him. She shook her head, glancing towards the bus stop before feeling in her pocket for her money.

Appallingly, it wasn't there. She remembered she had had a pound note, but she had taken it out of her pocket in the house when she reached for her handkerchief to dry her eyes. She glanced uncertainly towards it. She couldn't go back there now, not after. . . .

'Are you sure? I can put the hood down, and you can feel the breeze in your hair.'

'I. . . .' Should she tell him that she'd lost her bus fare? But what if he asked why she hadn't borrowed some from the friends she'd been visiting?

It would be a long walk back to the home— several miles, and they had no idea where she was.

'If you're sure it won't be any trouble?'

'On the contrary.'

There was an irony in the words that went over her head, and neither did she see the cynical smile he gave her as he opened the car door and pushed down the canvas hood.

As he had said, the cooling breeze was pleasant. He drove well, but Laurel was unprepared for him to stop suddenly in a quiet lane several minutes away from the home, and completely deserted.

Panic flared as he turned towards her. He seemed to have changed somehow, his face, which she dimly recognised as handsome, hardening.

'You're Laurel James, aren't you?' he demanded.

She didn't even think of lying. 'Yes,' she admitted huskily. 'Who are you?'

'Oliver Savage,' he told her briefly, but his name meant nothing to her then.

'How did you know it was me?'

'I recognised your picture. You were going to see your mother, weren't you?'

'Yes.' To her horror Laurel felt the tears filling her eyes and sliding helplessly down her cheeks. 'She hates me,' she blurted out, suddenly over-whelmed with pain and desolation. 'She said it was my fault. . . .'

'And wasn't it?'

Oliver Savage had turned towards her, one arm along the back of her seat, but there was nothing threatening about him, in fact he seemed to exude the same sort of dependability as her grandfather.

'I don't know.' Anguish and pain mingled in the words. 'She says I encouraged him, but I didn't . . . I didn't!'

'Not even the tiniest little bit? You're a very attractive girl . . . very sexy too,' he said with a glimmer of a smile. 'Or rather you would be out of those baggy clothes. You must have known that he desired you?'

Laurel nodded. There was a certain amount of relief to be found in talking like this to a stranger, a certain catharsis, and all at once she was talking quickly, softly, words tumbling over each other as she told her story. He stopped her once or twice, asking questions, which she answered briefly. In many ways he wasn't there, he was simply a listening post, a substitute for the grandfather she loved; someone she could unburden herself to.

When it was over she was crying, softly and quietly. His fingers touched the back of her neck, drawing her head down against his shoulder. The contact with another human being was strangely comforting. The emotional storm had left her tired and drained, and the slow thud of his heart soothed her.

'Better now?' he asked at length. 'You're a pretty potent package, you know,' he added when selfconsciousness returned and she had moved away from him. And there was an oddly strained look to his mouth. 'I'd better get you back before *I'm* accused of rape myself!'

His words shocked her, reminding her of how little she knew about him, how foolishly trusting she had been, and she scrambled out of the car before he could stop her—not that he made any attempt to do so. The smile he gave her as he drove off disturbed her. There was something about it that frightened her.

When she got back to the home no one had missed her. Rachel came to see her to tell her that they were moving her to another home—an all-girls one this time, where they thought she would fit in better.

For the first time since the trial she didn't ask about her mother, and as Rachel told her parents that night over their evening meal, 'I think she's beginning to accept that her mother's deserted her, poor little scrap. That brute Trenchard ought to have been locked away for a lifetime—not simply six months!'

It was the weekend before Laurel knew the truth; a weekend that brought to light Oliver Savage's real identity in the shape of a colour supplement article about her; an article that purported to be a personal interview with Oliver Savage, in which he tore her reputation and everything she had said to him in shreds. 'Does any really innocent teenager accept a lift from a stranger and then proceed to practically invite him to make love to her?' And so it went on, and reading it Laurel was barely able to believe it. Haltingly she explained to Rachel what had actually happened; how Oliver Savage had twisted everything she had said, pounced on her own admission that she had known of her stepfather's desire, and according to him fanned it.

'The man must have a warped mind to do something like this!' Rachel stormed later, when Laurel had been sedated and put to bed. 'He's talked to Laurel, seen her—he's supposed to be an intelligent human being, can't he guess what sort of effect his article is going to have on her? The first human being she brings herself to confide in, and he does this to her!'

'He's a reporter,' Peter told her dryly, 'What do you expect? Although I agree it was bad luck on Laurel's part that she had to meet him when she was at her most vulnerable. He's renowned for his dislike of the present rape laws; claims that in ninety cases out of a hundred the men have been led on and aren't totally to blame. No doubt he was waiting there, hoping for an interview with Trenchard, instead he got Laurel, poor little kid!'

Being involved in a rape case was something that clung like mud all through your life if you let it, Laurel reflected as she folded the papers and put them away. Shortly after the trial her mother had died, and then Bill Trenchard had been killed in a car accident several months after he had been released from gaol. Over the years she had learned to bury the past so deeply that it could never be resurrected, but today Oliver Savage had reappeared in her life, ripping the tissue of scars from old wounds, making her relive the past, and he wanted to talk to her. Why? So that he could do a follow-up article? Victim of sexual attack, six years on? What was he hoping to find? That she had lovers by the score? Bitter laughter welled up inside her. Well, he was doomed to disappointment. No man had ever touched her since. How could she let them; how could she offer a decent, moral man the body that had been sullied by her stepfather's touch; a body that the world told her had actively encouraged that touch? Coming on top of her ordeal at the trial Oliver Savage's article had driven her completely into her shell. For months she had simply refused to talk to anyone, and looking back now she shuddered to realise how close she had come to insanity. But that was all behind her now, and just as long as she remembered to trust no one, to rely on no one, she would be safe.

A little to her surprise she slept reasonably well, without the nightmares which had plagued her after the article was published. Feeling thankful that it was a Saturday and she had the weekend to recover her composure, she ate her breakfast, made out a shopping list and set out for her local shops, as was her normal Saturday morning ritual. One of her weekly chores was the changing of her library books. She was an avid reader, and the girl behind the desk recognised her.

'Why don't you try this?' she suggested, proffering Laurel a book. Her hand shook as she took it and saw the name Jonathan Graves on the spine.

'No, I don't think so. . . .' she began, then changed her mind, and clutched at the book until her knuckles whitened. Perhaps she ought to read it? Perhaps it would give her a deeper insight into the man, a clue as to why he would want to see her.

When she got home she rushed feverishly through her chores, skipping lunch and unwilling to admit even to herself that it was because of the book.

To punish herself she made herself wait until evening, refusing to read the brief description inside the jacket, instead plunging straight into the story.

He was an excellent writer; and when, halfway through the book, she turned to the front again, she wasn't surprised to read that the story was based on some factual reporting he had done and then used as the basis for this story.

Every nuance of his main character's behaviour and actions was cleverly analysed, and as she read the book, Laurel was seized by the conviction that this was what he wanted to do to her. He wanted to use her as the material for one of his books. He wanted to destroy her all over again. Well, he wasn't going to. She wouldn't let him!

It was gone ten before she put the book down. She went into the kitchen to make herself a drink and as she did so she heard her doorbell ring. That in itself was a rare enough occurrence to make her stiffen slightly, her eyes widening as she registered the sound.

The door was securely bolted as always and without opening it she demanded huskily, 'Who's there?'

'Me—Oliver Savage,' came the uncompromising reply. 'Open the door like a good girl, Laurel, I want to speak to you.'

'Go away,' she whispered chokily. 'Go away!'

It had no effect. She might just as well have not spoken. 'Let me in!' he demanded. 'I'm quite prepared to break the damned door down if you don't, Laurel!'

She believed him. And she hated the way he said her name in that intimate way, as though he had the right to use it. Knowing the curiosity and conventionality of her neighbours, she opened the door with unsteady fingers before his presence outside her door attracted their attention. Her flat was quite small and he seemed to make it seem smaller, a tall dark figure clad in dark close-fitting trousers, and expensive cashmere sweater and a supple leather jacket which he tossed casually on to her small sofa.

'Very homely,' he approved, glancing swiftly round the room. 'Live here alone, do you?'

'No, I share it with half a dozen men,' she spat back at him. 'Of course I live here alone. Do you honestly think anyone would want to share with a notorious person like me?'

'Notorious?' He swung round, studying her thoughtfully. 'Is that how you think of yourself, Laurel? It's a word that's normally applied to criminals; to guilt. . . .'

'And isn't that what you made me?' she demanded, fingers curling painfully into her palms. Her heart was thudding painfully, her whole body trembling. What was he doing here? What did he want?

'Laurel, sit down, I want to talk to you. I got your address from your office, and I had intended to come and see you tomorrow, but I was driving past and I saw your light was on. . . .'

'And you just couldn't resist making the most of the opportunity,' she sneered bitterly. 'You're good at that, aren't you?'

For a moment she thought she saw a glimmer of pain in his eyes, but they left her face to search the room, coming to rest on his book. He picked it up.

'You've been reading this? Did you enjoy it?'

'Not half as much as you enjoyed destroying the main character,' she told him acidly, ignoring his small frown. 'But I won't let you do that to me— not again. You aren't going to use me for one of your novels!'

'That's what you think I intend to do?' He

shook his head as though he couldn't believe her. 'Laurel, it isn't like that. Look, come and sit down.'

He reached towards her and she backed away, her eyes unknowingly petrified, her voice high-pitched with fear and raised her hands to ward him off. 'Don't touch me!'

'I wasn't going to,' he told her tautly, 'at least, not in the way that you mean. Laurel, hasn't anyone ever told you that saying that to a man is the biggest come-on there is?'

She blenched and moaned a husky denial, all her normal reserve stripped from her by the combination of Oliver Savage's unexpected appearance and her own journey back to the past. He was telling her as he had told the world that she had willingly and knowingly encouraged her stepfather, and it wasn't true. It wasn't true!'

'Laurel.' He ignored her cowering rejection and gripped her shoulders, his face almost as pale as her own. 'Oh no, I didn't mean what you think.'

He was the first man to touch her in six years, and her body screamed a bitter protest and she tried to wrench herself free, panicking like a trapped animal.

'Laurel, listen to me.' One hand left her shoulder to circle her throat, tipping her head backwards so that she was forced to look up at him. She struggled to subdue her panic, the fear that his touch aroused.

'It's all right, I'm not going to hurt you.'

He bent towards her, his face shadowed, ignoring her frantic attempt to break free. The touch of his lips on hers transported her instanteously back through time. She was in the bathroom of her home with Bill Trenchard leaning over her, sickening her with the wine-sour scent of his breath. She opened her mouth to scream, her body rigid with terror, but Oliver Savage's mouth smothered the sound, his hand caressing her shoulders, his lips leaving her mouth to whisper against her ear, as though he had seen into her mind. 'Laurel, I'm not Trenchard. I won't hurt you.'

He released her slowly and carefully, drawing her with him towards the small sofa.

'I suppose now that you've discovered I'm frigid it rather spoils your story line,' she managed to get out in the thick silence that followed. 'No doubt it would suit you better to discover that I turned into a raving nymphomaniac!'

His quiet, 'I don't believe you're frigid, but I can see that you've done an excellent job of convincing yourself that you are,' cut through her bitter words.

'Why?' he asked her. 'For protection?'

He saw and guessed too much. Suddenly even breathing was a painful effort. She wanted to close her eyes and blot out the sight of his face; a face that had haunted her nightmares long after she had begun to forget Bill Trenchard's. Why he should have such a cataclysmic effect upon her she wasn't sure. Perhaps it was because he had caught her at her most vulnerable, offered her comfort and understanding, only to betray her and reveal all her innermost fears and thoughts in his article.

'Don't you think I need it?' she asked huskily at last. 'Have you any idea what it's like to be me? To be rejected by your own mother; to be treated like a whore? I hope you're proud of what you've done!'

'What I've done?' The grey eyes were blank. 'I can't give you back the lost years, Laurel, I didn't even think I could make atonement, but after tonight. . . .' He seemed lost in his thoughts, his eyes resting for several seconds on his book, and then he said abruptly, 'Have you anything to drink? Anything other than tea or coffee, I mean,' he elaborated sardonically.

'There's a bottle of sherry.' She coloured as he pulled a wry face, and said defensively, 'I don't drink.'

'And you don't entertain gentlemen callers,' he added for her. 'Very well, perhaps I should have thought of that and had a couple before I came here,'

So there were some things that even the Oliver Savages of this world needed Dutch courage for!

'I won't allow you to use me as the basis for one of your books, Mr Savage,' she told him primly.

'Who's asking you to? Oh, for Pete's sake!' Angry fingers disturbed the thickness of his dark hair. 'Laurel, I haven't come here to coerce you into agreeing to feature in one of my books. It's got nothing to do with anything like that. I've been looking for you for the last five years—I've had notices in the papers; everything. Understandably perhaps, the social services wouldn't tell me where you were, but I thought once you'd left whatever home they'd sent you to, you might be curious or angry enough to get in touch with me.'

'Home?' she queried cynically, anger spilling past her fear and reserve to colour her eyes dark amber. 'Don't you mean institution, because that's what they are. Places where they send difficult or damaged children; places. . . .'

'Laurel!'

For one incredible moment she thought she saw bitter anguish in his eyes and it was enough to stop her in mid-sentence, her eyes widening slightly. He was quick to take advantage of her silence.

'Laurel, I know the truth.'

'I know you do,' she agreed bitterly. 'I told it to you, but that didn't stop you distorting it to make a name for yourself, did it?'

'Please, just listen to me, will you? Nothing can excuse what I did to you—I admit that. I tried to get a different side of your story published, but by that time it was old news and my paper wouldn't take it, and anyway, by that time your stepfather was dead and with him any proof that he'd lied.

'When I saw you coming out of your house that day I was waiting for him. We had an appointment. We'd already talked once and I'd got an exclusive from him—My sympathies lay with him at that time, I'm not going to deny that. You see, a young cousin of mine had got himself involved with a girl a couple of years before—his parents were very strict; very moral.

'Lisa was an opportunist. She met him, seduced him and then tried to blackmail him when he told her the affair was over. You see, she knew he came from a wealthy background; she wanted to force him into marrying her and when he wouldn't she accused him of rape. She won the case, by lying through her teeth, but she was an excellent actress, and Bobby didn't come across well at all. His parents refused to have anything to do with him. They were shocked and disgusted. He was sentenced to gaol, but he committed suicide before his sentence started. He told me everything the night before the trial, and later, when he was dead, Lisa admitted the truth to me.'

Glancing up into his shuttered face, Laurel shivered, trying to imagine just how he had dragged the truth from the other girl, who sounded as hard and selfish as her stepfather.

'So rightly or wrongly, what happened to him made me biased against the victims of rape cases. It isn't exactly unheard-of for a girl to use the threat as a means of getting money out of some poor male.'

'Meaning you thought I wanted money from my stepfather?' Laurel demanded disbelievingly.

'Not money—but I thought you might be using the threat as a weapon. Look at it from another angle, Laurel. Your mother marries again, and you become a third in the family triangle. Naturally you're jealous; naturally also as a teenager you're becoming more and more aware of yourself as a woman; it's only natural that you should want to test those burgeoning powers; all girls do, and what could be more natural than that you should test them on your stepfather; tease him a little, perhaps?'

'No!'

The husky denial and the shudder that followed it darkened his eyes.

'No,' Oliver agreed sombrely, 'but I didn't know that until it was too late. When I saw you that afternoon and you accepted a lift in my car without even knowing who I was——'

'I'd left my bus fare in the house,' Laurel broke in briefly. 'My mother had just told me . . . just said that she never wanted to see me again. I couldn't go back, and. ... .' She closed her mouth firmly. She wasn't going to betray to him the fact that she had felt drawn to him, had trusted him. A fierce wave of hatred washed over her. Six years ago he had been instrumental in destroying her life, as much to blame in her eyes as her stepfather. Bill Trenchard was now dead and beyond reach,

but this man. . . . Feverish thoughts chased one
another through her mind as she listened to him,
her lips burning where his had touched them. How
dared he presume to touch her, to walk into her
life calmly saying that he was wrong and expecting
her to accept his apology? All the emotions she
had dammed up for so long welled to the surface
and she was consumed by a violent need to make
Oliver Savage suffer as she had done; to hold him
to public ridicule and private torment.

'Laurel, are you listening to me?'

She had had six long years to perfect the ability
to conceal her emotions, and nothing of her
thoughts showed in her expression as she nodded
her head.

'Just after your stepfather had completed his
sentence I ran into him in a Fleet Street
pub—just one of those odd quirks of fate. He'd
been drinking heavily, and he recognised me. I
suppose when I first interviewed him I had
sensed that my sympathies lay with him, because
it wasn't long before he was boasting to me how
he'd fooled the court; how he'd deliberately lied
about you.'

It was no more than Laurel had known
instinctively all along, but instead of feeling
vindicated, all she could feel was a terrible burning
anger.

'He was killed three days later,' Oliver Savage
told her broodingly, 'Before I could get him to
sign any statement.'

'It wouldn't have done any good anyway,'
Laurel said lightly. 'My life could never have been
the same. You see, it was my mother who found
him with me, and she preferred to believe that the
fault lay with me rather than him. I was taken into
care for my own protection, not punishment—all

that was carefully explained to me, but it amounts to the same thing in the end.'

She wasn't going to tell him of her mental anguish; of her pain and self-hatred, all engendered by the belief that somehow she had invited what had happened to her; that somehow she was wicked and sinful and that she was to blame. They had explained carefully to her that she was not, that she was punishing herself for a crime she had never committed and that one day she would be able to accept this. But she hadn't done. The tiny seeds of doubt had been sown and they had grown into weeds of monstrous proportions, and now the man who was directly responsible for some of them was sitting here calmly in her sitting room telling her that he was sorry and that it had been a mistake!

She looked up at him, on the point of asking him to leave, surprising an expression in his eyes and a tautness of his mouth that was like a red rag to a bull. Pity! How dared he pity her! Pity was the thing she had come to loathe and resent the most in the long lonely years. Pity was not always what it seemed. How often had she discovered it masked prurient, avid curiosity about what had happened.

Her throat thick with anger that threatened to choke her, she felt the black, swirling mists of the past possess her. A rage she could almost taste and smell enveloped her, burning through her body. How dared he sit there so arrogantly saying he had made a mistake, and expecting her simply to forgive and forget? Was he blind? Obtuse? Didn't he realise that he had helped to virtually destroy her life? Her pain was like a living, caged animal straining for release. How could she convey with mere words the depths of the anguish and humiliation she had known? The degradation of self-doubt and self-hatred she had lived with? To understand he would have to experience them for himself.

He reached out towards her, covering her clenched folded hands with the warmth of his, and his touch was like burning acid. A murderous fury exploded inside her. How dared he patronise her with his compassion, with the pity she could see quite plainly in his eyes?

She wanted to lash out; to hurt and degrade him as he had done her.

'Laurel, if there's anything I can do to make amends?'

Had she actually heard those quiet, calm words? Did he honestly think there was anything he could do to right the wrongs of the past? Was he a magician, could he turn back time and make her the innocent happy teenager she had once been?

She opened her mouth to tell him hotly that there was nothing; nothing he could do; nothing she would ever accept from him; that she would die rather than accept so much as a crust from him, when a tiny ice-cold inner voice stilled the hot words.

What if it were not mere chance that had brought them together again, but—for want of a better word—fate! Fate giving her a chance to turn the tables on him, to exact from him payment for all that she had endured.

As soon as the thought was born she dismissed it as sheer impossibility. How could she possibly do anything that could make him suffer a tithe of what she had endured? He was a man of thirty-odd, fully armoured and protected against what-ever puny blows she could deal him, but the mad urge to escape from the pity she had seen so fleetingly in his glance fuelled her imagination, lending it a potency that she barely recognised. There must be a way, it insisted; everyone had their Achilles heel, and Oliver Savage would be no different. All she had to do was find it. But how? What did he cherish most in his life? A woman? She dismissed the thought almost immediately. He was too self-contained, too much in control to be vulnerable in that way. Then what?

In a Machiavellian flash of enlightenment it came to her. His career. His precious career! The career which he had furthered by using her! She expelled her pent-up breath, slowly, her mouth curving in a smile which brought a frown to the eyes of the man watching her. Poetic justice! Almost she breathed the words out aloud. A strange fevered urgency had taken possession of her, almost at the exact moment his hand had closed over hers, awakening memories she refused to admit were still there; memories that were encapsulated in the dreams she sometimes still had of being held safe and warm in arms that held the rest of the world at bay; but those dreams always gave way to the same nightmare; the same terror that engulfed her, plunging her into pain and fear.

Tension spiralled nervously through her, her mind working overtime as it raced to discover a means of putting into action her plan. With cool clarity a thought took root in her mind and grew. Oliver Savage had written lies about her, had twisted the truth and used her. She must find a way of subjecting him to the same humiliation; of destroying his credibility among his colleagues. For several months she had been attending a creative writing course at her local night-school. She enjoyed the classes, and had been told she showed promise. What if she could find some way of discrediting her enemy in an article?

Several pitfalls leapt to mind almost immediately. First she would have to discover something she could use against Oliver Savage, and secondly she would have to persuade someone to publish it. The gutter-press were always anxious to publish articles about well-known personalities she realised quickly, she could. . . .

What? an inner voice mocked. Make something up? No, that would never do; there were laws about such things, and besides, she wanted the satisfaction of knowing she had used the truth. There must be something in the life of a man like Oliver Savage that he wouldn't want made public, surely, but what? And how was she likely to discover it? Simply by asking him? No, to learn something of real value meant getting a lot closer to her quarry than she was now. Her glance flickered over him. He was watching her, and prickles of awareness shivered over her skin, almost as though he had physically reached out and touched her. Laurel shuddered, feeling her hatred of him burning her skin. For years she had almost been successful in putting him out of her mind and now, suddenly, all her hatred and bitterness had come boiling to the surface, demanding satisfaction.

'There is something,' she said huskily, at last. 'I'm very anxious to further my career. If I work as your secretary for a few months, then I'm sure with your recommendation I could get a first-class job. . . .'

He was watching her closely, frowning, and her heart pounded with fear that he might have guessed her underlying motive.

'Why bother working for me?' he demanded. 'Why not simply ask me for a recommendation?'

Her face tight, she said coldly, 'Because that

would be dishonest, but if you didn't mean what you said. . . .'

She was amazed at her own ability; her hitherto unknown talent for finding a raw spot.

'I don't normally employ a secretary,' he told her curtly, 'I use a dictating machine, and besides. . . .'

'You don't want a frigid female like me working for you?' Laurel suggested acidly, knowing that her accusation would remind him of just why she was frigid.

'Frigid? I've already told you, I don't believe. . . .' He broke off and seemed lost in a brown study for several seconds. Laurel wondered what he was thinking; if he was regretting his offer to make reparation. Perhaps he had expected her simply to accept his apology and then let him leave.

'That's really what you want? To work for me?'

'To work for you with a view to getting some useful references for the future,' Laurel corrected, again marvelling at her ability to act.

'You're obviously a good secretary, and I am just about to start on a new book. Besides. . . . Very well,' he said curtly. 'But I hope you have a passport.'

'A passport?' She was stunned. 'But. . . .'

'I have a farmhouse in Provence where I do my writing,' he told her blandly. 'It's extremely remote and there'll just be the two of us there. Think you can cope?'

Could she? Could she cope with the physical presence of this man on an intimate daily basis? Intimacy worked two ways, she reminded herself, there was no knowing what confidences Oliver Savage might make as they worked, not guessing what he might reveal. He had not led the life of a monk; she was aware of that. Already in her mind's eye she could see the headlines, 'Well-known writer's secret life'—and there must be a secret, something she could find and twist as he had done with her. There must be!

Squaring her shoulders, she said confidently, 'I can cope.'

'At least there's one thing I won't have to worry about,' Oliver Savage commented dryly as he made for the door. 'You aren't likely to use the situation to promote any other sort of intimacy between us, are you? Have you never felt the slightest bit of curiosity about what it would be like to make love with someone?' he questioned as she opened the door for him.

'Never,' she told him coldly, dull colour burning up under her skin, as she added for good measure, 'I find the thought totally revolting!'

'Then perhaps it's time that someone taught you differently,' were his last words as she closed the door behind him.

How dared he pity her! she seethed angrily when he had gone—because there had been pity, as well as something else, in the final glance he had given her just before he left. But soon he would have no room to pity anyone but himself. She would see to that!

CHAPTER FOUR

ONCE his mind was made up Oliver moved with breathtaking speed, as Laurel soon discovered. By subtle flattery he managed to persuade Mr Marshall to release her on a mere week's notice. Sally goggled when she heard the news, exclaiming disbelievingly, 'You're going to work for Oliver Savage? Oh, Laurel what a waste! If I were in your shoes. . . .'

'You'd be thinking more about going to bed with him than working for him,' Laurel guessed accurately, shocking Sally a little, as she wasn't used to hearing Laurel speak so frankly. 'Why do you think he's employing me?' she asked with a certain amount of grim amusement. 'He wants a secretary, Sally, not a bedmate.'

'No,' Sally agreed unthinkingly. 'Not that I imagine he has much difficulty in finding the latter. Still, I think you're very lucky,' she added wistfully. 'Provence. . . .'

Not so much lucky as quick-thinking, Laurel told herself three days later as she presented herself at Oliver's London apartment as per his instructions.

It was in a luxurious but surprisingly discreet block not far from the city centre. He opened the door to her himself, clad only in a towel wrapped carelessly round his hips. His mouth quirked in amusement at her horrified expression, his eyebrows lifting slightly as he explained, 'I had rather a late night, and as a consequence. . . .'

'Don't bother to explain,' Laurel cut in. 'I can imagine.'

'You can?' This time his voice and expression were both sardonic. 'You surprise me. I didn't realise you knew what working through the night can do to you. Somehow I didn't imagine they went in for that sort of thing in accountants' offices—I thought they were strictly nine to five. Still, it makes it easier if you do know, then you won't be surprised if I ask you to take dictation in the evenings occasionally, will you?'

Laurel hadn't for a moment meant that he had spent the night working, and they both knew it. Her face tight, she stepped past him into the hall. It was painted in a soft shade of green, cool and relaxing, but her overall impression of the large living room he led her to was that while it was expensive and effective it wasn't a homely room, and she thought nostalgically of the house in Hampstead as it had been when her grandparents were still alive.

'I'm flying to Nice a day ahead of schedule,' Oliver explained to her as he gestured to her to sit down. 'I want you to type up some letters for me—you can sign them per pro. I've told the staff that you'll be working here for a day. I've got something to do in Nice, but it won't take long.'

Laurel wished he would go away and get dressed. The sight of his body clad only in that brief towel was disturbing her. Since her teens she had been unable to look at a male body without feeling revulsion and loathing, and yet for some reason her eyes were drawn to Oliver's almost against her will.

'You're going to have to stop looking at me like that if we're going to work successfully together, you know,' he told her dryly, watching the colour flood her face. 'I know how you feel about me, Laurel, but I'm not your stepfather.'

She bent her head over the notebook in her lap. 'I know.' The shaky admission was forced reluctantly past her lips.

'Do you?'

She was aware of him moving, coming to stand beside her, but a strange weakness held her in thrall. Her body tensed at his proximity. She hated him and she wanted to tell him so.

'Prove it to me, Laurel,' he commanded softly. 'Look at me.'

What was he trying to do? What was he trying to prove?

She wanted to tell him that she couldn't, but she refused to expose her weakness to him. With an effort of will that left her strangely shaky she managed to focus her eyes on his face.

'Look at my body, Laurel,' he told her insistently. 'It isn't something to be afraid of. It's only muscle and flesh.' Before she could stop him he lifted her palm and placed it against his bare shoulder. 'See?'

Her breath seemed to be dammed up in her throat, her fingers trembling where they had touched his skin. She wanted to withdraw from him, but he wouldn't let her, his eyes holding hers.

'It isn't so bad, Laurel, is it?' he demanded softly as she shivered and trembled, unable to move.

She wanted to move away, but she seemed rooted to the spot, her fingers curling into his flesh as he moved closer, trapping her in his arms, his eyes steely grey as they looked down into hers, and she tried to move away.

'Your heart is thudding like jungle drums,' he told her. 'What are you frightened of, Laurel?'

He was holding her quite loosely, not really imprisoning her at all. 'I thought you were going to kiss me,' she admitted huskily, unable to stop her trembling lips from admitting the truth.

'So I was,' Oliver agreed pleasantly, his eyes narrowing over her disturbed features. 'Is that such a dreadful thing?'

'You know I don't like it.' The words sounded childishly petulant, and she couldn't believe she had uttered them; had spoken so frankly to him.

'Don't?' he queried. 'Or won't let yourself? It can be very enjoyable, if you'd just let yourself enjoy it. There's no sin in kissing someone, Laurel—look, I'll show you.' There was a look in his eyes she couldn't interpret.

This time she kept her mouth tightly closed, but it didn't appear to bother him. His lips moved gently over hers, brushing them lightly until her sensitised flesh reacted to the light contact. Against her will her lips softened and some of the rigidity left her body, but when Oliver's tongue stroked the passive outline of her mouth it awoke all her dormant fears, and she sprang away from him, her eyes wild and frightened.

'Why did you do that?' she demanded bitterly. 'You know I don't like it.'

'You think you don't,' he corrected briefly. 'As to why—call it atonement, if you have to give a name to it.'

Atonement ... what on earth did he mean by that? she asked herself blankly when he disappeared, telling her that he was going to get dressed.

When he returned he was dressed in jeans and sweater, the latter moulded firmly to the muscles of his chest and back, and Laurel found her mind wandering against her will to the smoothness of his skin beneath her fingers. His body wasn't like Bill Trenchard's. It was smooth and golden brown,

lightly sprinkled with dark hair. Unknowingly
Laurel pressed her fingers to her lips still quivering
from his touch. Just for a moment with his lips
brushing hers she had felt . . . had felt . . . what?

That weak sensation coursing through her must
have been an offshoot of her hatred of him.

Two days later she was in Nice. Oliver met her at
the airport, looking oddly different in frayed jeans
and a thin cotton tee-shirt. It was at least fifteen
degrees warmer than it had been in London.
Spring was already well advanced, and Laurel felt
over-warm in the heavyweight winter coat she had
worn for the flight. A stewardess gave them an
odd look as she walked past them—wondering
what on earth such a plain creature was doing with
someone like Oliver Savage, Laurel acknowledged
mentally as she followed him out into the brilliant
sunshine.

'This way.' His hand on her shoulder directed
her towards the dark, menacing outline of a
Ferrari, parked on the forecourt.

'This is all the luggage you've brought?' he
asked as she handed him her single, old-fashioned
suitcase.

'You said the farmhouse was remote,' Laurel
reminded him. 'And as you'll be busy on the book,
I've only brought work things with me.'

'You mean you actually do go out?' He sounded
disbelieving. 'But not with men, eh, Laurel?'

She had the impression that he was deliberately
baiting her, and resisted the impulse to react.
Perhaps he was regretting giving her the job. Well,
she wasn't going to give him the opportunity to
send her back now.

When he had said the farmhouse was remote,
she hadn't realised to what extent. It was late

afternoon before they reached it, set amidst ancient olives, the terracotta building faded and softened by the sun.

'Out you get.'

She was stiff from the long drive and stumbled as she clambered out of the car. Instantly Oliver was at her side, grasping her waist to steady her, only the shock of the physical contact had her trembling like a leaf, her face milk-white as she stared blindly away from the tanned column of his throat.

'And to think I thought I was making progress!' she thought she heard him mutter as he released her and bent down to pick up her case.

'This way,' he instructed, leaving her to follow him through what had once been a garden, but was now a tangle of roses and hollyhocks mingling with almost knee-high grass.

'As you can see, I don't get much time for gardening,' Oliver told her wryly, correctly reading her expression. 'But then I came down here to write, not till the land.'

He pushed open the door, standing aside so that Laurel could precede him into the cool shadowy kitchen, which was obviously the heart of the farmhouse.

Ancient tiles covered the floor, dusty and neglected, another film of dust covered the dresser and cupboards. The room smelled musty, and Laurel wondered how long it had been since Oliver had last visited it.

'Let's get some of these windows open and then I'll show you round. Fortunately we do have electricity—although it's supplied by our own generator. I'll go and get it going in a minute, and then if you will you can stock the freezer with the stuff I've got in the boot. I hope you're not going to object to mucking in a bit with the chores,' he added as he stretched up to open one of the windows. 'I know it's not part of the normal secretarial duties. . . .'

'I don't mind.' There was no point in antagonising him at this stage, and who knew, perhaps during the shared intimacy of doing the dishes she might learn something she could use against him later.

'Good girl! Come on then, I'll give you the full tour. Not that there's much to see,' he added as he bent his head to avoid the lintel of the doorway that led from the kitchen to what was obviously the living room.

Pleasantly proportioned, it had windows looking out on both the front and back of the property. Like the kitchen, it looked dusty and forlorn, but it was comfortably furnished with typical Provençal furniture. There was a huge open fireplace at one end, and an enormous desk, tidy now, but obviously Oliver used the room as his study. Behind the desk ran a series of bookshelves, full mainly of reference and textbooks, from what Laurel could see.

'Upstairs now. It's a little larger than the downstairs,' Oliver explained as he led the way up the narrow twisting flight of stairs. 'Mainly because it's been extended out over what was the barn and what is now the garage-cum-storeroom.

'Five bedrooms.' He pushed open the doors of each of them in turn. 'This one's mine.' It contained an old-fashioned bed with wooden head board and a heavy but attractive armoire.

'You can take your choice of the other four. Bathroom has to be shared, I'm afraid. We're a little primitive in these parts, none of the luxuries of civilisation.'

'There's no lock on the door,' Laurel said jerkily, her eyes flying to his face.

'I've never felt the need to lock myself in,' came the cool response. 'I'm no peeping Tom, Laurel,' he added impatiently. 'If I want to see a naked woman I don't have to go peering into bathrooms to do so.'

She flushed at the sardonic tone, and accepted his suggestion that she have the room at the head of the stairs. When she had decided to be revenged upon him she had overlooked the problem of her aversion to men and their enforced promixity.

'It's larger than the others—and further away from mine, which should make you feel safer,' Oliver told her. 'Tell me,' he enquired silkily, 'if you're so terrified that I might touch you why did you suggest working with me? Was it purely because you wanted to advance your career?'

Because she couldn't answer the question without lying and because she was wary of the look in his eyes, Laurel put a question of her own.

'Why did you accept me?' she asked lightly.

'Well now. . . .' Oliver was watching her in a curious fashion, and all of a sudden her mouth went dry, her heart thudding erratically. 'I wondered when we'd get to this. What would you say if I told you that I feel guilty about what's happened to you, Laurel? About your fear and loathing of men—No, don't deny it, we both know it's there, and in some part I'm to blame. I want to help you, Laurel.' If she didn't know it wasn't possible she might almost have suspected there was gentleness in his voice, compassion in his eyes as they rested on her pale face.

'What did you say?' She stared at him in mingled fury and outrage.

'You don't like the idea?' he guessed, grimacing

faintly. 'Ah well, I didn't think you would—but, Laurel, think, do you really want to go through the rest of your life terrified of men and sex? Do you. . . .?'

'I'm not!'

'Oh no?' His mouth was wry. 'My dear girl, I could take you to my bed right here and now and make love to you, but we both know that before I got half a dozen steps you'd be halfway to fainting with terror. I know what happened to you wasn't pleasant, but it's over, Laurel, you've got to learn to live.' That couldn't be anguish she thought she saw in his eyes, it was just a trick of the light. But he would know anguish!

'And you're going to teach me? No way! I'm leaving here right now. Oh, I might have known you'd have some ulterior motive, some reason for giving me the job. I suppose you're going to write about it as well,' she demanded sarcastically. '"How I single-handed turned a frigid woman of ice into a raging sexpot . . .".' Dear God, if she'd dreamed this would be in his mind, she would never have suggested working for him—retribution or not!

Oliver's reactions were far too swift. 'So you admit it can be done,' he pounced triumphantly. 'But no, I don't intend to write about it, Laurel. You seem to have a fixation about that—why?'

'Perhaps because I've experienced your written words!'

'Yes, you have, haven't you?' His face tightened. 'Laurel, I. . . .' he moved towards her, checking when she flinched, to say in a hard voice, 'I meant every word I said, Laurel. By the time we leave here in the autumn my book will be finished and you'll be a feeling, living woman.'

'I will? I didn't realise you could perform

miracles,' she sniped back at him bitterly. 'Do I get to know just how you're going to affect this transformation?'

He shrugged powerful shoulders. 'I wish I knew, but it will be accomplished, Laurel, I promise you that. After all, I owe it to you to give you back what you keep on reminding me I took from you, don't I?' She could feel the heat of his anger beneath the suave exterior.

He left before she could retort, and as she heard his feet clattering down the narrow stairs Laurel sank down on to the unmade bed, her heart pounding nervously.

She shouldn't have come here. She had let her desire for revenge blind her to the dangers. What did Oliver mean, he was going to turn her into a feeling woman? How did he expect to do that? She shivered shuddenly, remembering the touch of his mouth against hers, and the way he had looked at her afterwards. She should never have agreed to come here. But she had, and she had a mission to accomplish, and if Oliver thought he could undo the harm he had helped to cause all those years ago, then let him try; she knew differently.

She was just searching for bedlinen when she heard him coming back upstairs.

'Generator's going,' he told her. 'We'd better get all that stuff in the freezer, before it thaws.'

They worked in relative harmony for half an hour. Watching Oliver work was a revelation. Her stepfather hadn't so much as lifted a finger in the house, and her grandmother had been the old-fashioned sort who never allowed her husband in the kitchen.

When they had finished, it was Oliver who pushed her down into a chair and told her to sit there while he made them a drink.

'Tea okay?' he asked her, filling the kettle. 'I'll go out and fill the pool later—we can use it once the sun's warmed it up.'

'The pool?' Laurel stared at him.

'Yes, there's a swimming pool down by the orchard. It was installed by the painter who owned the house before me. He used it to lure nubile young ladies up here and then coaxed them into posing for him in the nude. Oh, for Pete's sake!' he exclaimed when he saw her shocked expression. 'I'm only joking—the pool was installed by a painter, but so far as I know it wasn't used by anyone except his four kids. You've got a very lurid imagination for a supposedly frigid young woman. What goes on inside that head of yours, Laurel? Why did you really come down here with me?'

'You know why,' she told him in a muffled voice.

'I know what you told me,' he corrected, switching off the kettle and pouring the water into the pot. 'But something tells me it isn't the truth, or at least not all of it.'

Had he guessed her real reason for coming with him? Surely not? She darted a hesitant glance towards him and then looked away. He couldn't have guessed. He would never have given her the job if he had.

'It's all right, Laurel,' he told her drily, 'You can look at me without me pouncing on you, you know. You must be hot in that outfit,' he commented, suddenly changing the subject, glancing casually at her tweed-suited figure and heavy shoes. 'Have you brought anything lighter with you?'

She had—two linen suits and the staid court shoes she wore during the summer for work.

'A swimsuit?' he queried, grimacing slightly as she coloured. 'No, of course not, I don't suppose you possess such a thing, do you?'

'I didn't know there was a pool,' she said evasively.

'And of course nothing in this world would persuade you to swim totally nude. Not even if I were to tell you that the kiss of the water against your skin is the most erotic sensation in the world, after the kiss of a lover's body, of course.'

Laurel was aware that hectic patches of colour stained her cheeks, Her head bent and her voice husky, she pleaded, 'You shouldn't talk to me like that.'

'Why not? Do you find it ... disturbing? You shouldn't—you're frigid, remember?'

'I find it ... disgusting!' Laurel spat back at him. 'Perhaps your women friends enjoy being spoken to like that, but. . . .'

'It isn't conversation my "woman friends" as you're pleased to call them want from me, Laurel,' Oliver told her softly, watching the colour come and go in her face. There was a small, electric pause.

'Come on,' he said abruptly. 'We won't be able to get any work done tonight, but at least we can make the place habitable. I hope you weren't expecting luxury and a cleaning staff laid on? We get deliveries once a week from the local town, but that's the limit, and I don't intend to waste precious time on shopping trips. Which do you prefer to do? Making the beds or doing the dusting?'

'I'll make the beds,' Laurel offered, avoiding his eyes as they glowed with mocking awareness of her disturbed emotions as he showed her where the bedlinen was stored. As he bent down to open the

chest the nape of his neck was exposed, oddly
vulnerable in some way, and she had a sudden
urge to reach down and touch the thick glossy
hair. An urge she subdued in appalled horror, only
too aware of Oliver's mocking reaction if he were
to glance upwards and see what she had been
feeling.

She couldn't understand herself, she reflected an
hour later, as she finished washing the patterned
china off the dresser. Hitherto she had hated and
loathed all men, dreading their touch, hating them
to come anywhere near her, and yet she had
experienced both curiosity and an urge to touch
Oliver's body. She couldn't understand it, and she
told herself it was a natural result of her desire to
be revenged upon him. After all, how was she
going to be able to find his weak points if she
didn't get to know him?

With that in mind she studied him covertly over
their evening meal. Oliver, much to her surprise,
had insisted on preparing them an omelette and
salad, both of which Laurel found she was
enjoying. She watched him as he ate, each
movement sparing and controlled, unlike her
stepfather, who had been wont to eat greedily.

He hadn't aged much in the last six years. If
anything his features were harder, leaner, that was
all.

'Tired?'

She hadn't realised that while she studied him,
he had been watching her.

'A little,' she admitted, 'but there's still the
washing up and I haven't unpacked.' With a start
she remembered that her case was still in the car.

'I'll go and get it for you,' Oliver announced
when she mentioned this, 'but don't bother
unpacking tonight,' he advised her. 'Leave it until

tomorrow. We won't start work for a couple of days. I've got some reading up to do, and it could take you a while to work off the effects of the journey, especially if you intend to walk around dressed for the Arctic,' he added, giving her tweed suit a cynical glance. 'Why do you do it, Laurel?' he asked. 'A way of repelling all boarders, like the hairstyle all scraped back and severe?'

He saw too much, knew too much, and it frightened her.

'I. . . . It's tidy,' she said defensively, her hand going instinctively to her sleek chignon. 'I prefer it like this.' She had a vivid memory of how she had looked in court, her hair all wild and untidy, and how the jury had reacted. 'It suits me better.'

'You think so?' For a moment Oliver's eyes were oddly compassionate. 'You go on up to bed, I'll get your case and leave it on the landing—and, Laurel . . .' She looked up at him. 'There's plenty of hot water if you want a bath, and I promise you you won't be disturbed.'

She gave him a cold glare. Of course she wouldn't be disturbed. She knew very well she was hardly likely to appear desirable in the eyes of a man like Oliver Savage, and with the knowledge for some reason came a tiny shaft of pain, as though there was something to regret in that fact.

Later, drowsy and on the edge of sleep, she found herself remembering that tiny shaft of pain, remembering and questioning it, but she was asleep before she could find an answer.

CHAPTER FIVE

THE sun streaming in through her window eventually woke her, too strong to be restrained by the thin curtains. It took her a few seconds to remember where she was, and then she glanced at her watch in dismay, sensing that she had overslept.

It was half-past nine. Oliver had said that they wouldn't start work immediately, but he had mentioned sharing the chores, and for all she knew that meant her getting the breakfast.

She remembered the meal he had prepared the previous evening and how much she had enjoyed it. She couldn't ever remember feeling so relaxed in the company of another human being, and yet underlying the relaxation had been a frisson of excitement. An awareness of him as a person—as a man!

She was letting her imagination run away with her, she scolded herself; any excitement she might have felt had its roots in her determination to be revenged upon Oliver for the past. She groped towards the end of the bed for the thick, quilted housecoat she had brought with her, then remembered that she hadn't got as far as unpacking it. She looked round for her case, sure that she had left it beside the bed, but now it seemed to have vanished.

'Lost something?' Oliver drawled from the door. He held a cup of steaming fragrant coffee in one had, the other propping him up against the door frame. Hastily averting her eyes from the dark vee of flesh exposed by the unbuttoned neck of his shirt, Laurel nodded her head.

'My case. I'm sure I put it by the bed last night. . . .'

'So you did,' he agreed, sauntering easily into her room and placing the coffee beside her bed. 'And I removed it—after you'd gone to sleep.'

'You. . . .' For a moment Laurel thought she must have misheard him.

'I removed it,' he repeated softly. 'Shall I tell you why? You're dressing like a woman of fifty plus, Laurel, hiding your body behind a barrier of unenchanting clothes. I've already told you why I brought you here. . . .'

'So that you could turn me into a woman,' she agreed bitterly, forgetting her determination not to antagonise him. The sense of wellbeing with which she had awoken was totally destroyed, and she shrank instinctively further down the bed as Oliver stretched out lazily and flipped back the covers, grimacing at the prim plainness of her thick cotton nightdress, which enveloped her from head to foot.

'What am I suppose to do?' she demanded huskily, not wanting to meet his eyes; not wanting to witness the derision she knew must be in them. 'Wear this all the time I'm here?'

'Hardly,' he replied dryly. 'It's even worse than that obnoxious tweed suit. No, my dear Laurel, you will wear the clothes I bought for you in Nice when I arrived. Oh, please don't thank me,' he drawled mockingly when her mouth fell open. 'Call it a small recompense for past . . . errors. Don't you want to see what I bought you?'

An inner instinct warned her that he was being deliberately provocative; that he expected her to react, and so she was doing, her body quivering in fierce indignation, and pain too. With a jolt she realised that his condemnation of her clothes had hurt, and he had been right, she admitted bleakly. She had used her clothes as a barrier. Her clothes and her hairstyle. . . . Her hands went automatically to her hair, thick and loose.

'Leave it,' Oliver instructed as she started to screw it up on top of her head. His fingers covered hers, but his eyes weren't on her hair, they were on the taut thrust of her breasts, their shape outlined by the movement of her arms, and a hot wave of colour flooded over her body, as just for a moment his glanced stripped her of the camouflage of her nightgown, And then nausea followed embarrassment as she remembered how her stepfather had looked at her, his features transposing themselves on Oliver's.

'Laurel!'

His voice held a command she couldn't ignore. It was as though he knew what had happened and was determined not to let her confuse him with her stepfather.

'Laurel, look at me.' His voice was husky and compelling.

'I don't want your clothes,' she told him bitterly, using her anger to stamp out other, less understandable emotions.

'Oh yes, you do,' he contradicted softly, 'and if need be I'll dress you in them myself. You're a woman, Laurel,' he goaded her. 'Aren't you even the slightest bit curious? Don't you ever wonder what it would be like to have a man look at your body with love?'

'With lust, don't you mean?' she shot back at him. 'And I know what it's like!'

'Laurel, all men aren't like your stepfather.

Surely you can accept that? Surely you can take that first step towards freedom?'

'Freedom?' She looked up at him, and she sighed.

'You're trapped in a cage, Laurel,' he told her, 'and the only way out is by learning to trust, to believe that all men aren't like your stepfather.' He spoke quietly, intently, almost sincerely, but of course he couldn't be sincere, she knew that.

'Perhaps I like my cage,' she returned doggedly. 'Perhaps it's safer inside than out.'

'Cages are lonely, stultifying places, Laurel,' he warned her slowly. 'Outside you can breathe clean air, experience everything that life has to offer. It may not be safe and it may not be protective, but it's a damned sight better than slowly dying of cowardice. Now, drink your coffee, and I'll show you what I've bought for you.'

He was treating her like a child, Laurel thought impotently, overruling every objection she raised by the simple expedient of ignoring them, and she was completely at his mercy. Was this what he had had in mind all along? She ought to have listened to him when he told her how long he had been looking for her. Ought to have thought less about retribution and more about his motives for agreeing so readily to her suggestion that she work for him.

'Is this what you had in mind all along?' she demanded tautly as he passed her the coffee cup. 'Turning me back into a woman, freeing me from the past?'

'No, because I didn't know how it had affected you. Initially I merely wanted to apologise, but when I saw you—You said yourself that I was partially to blame, Laurel. I'm a man who always pays his debts. . . .'

'And if I don't want this one paid?'

'Oh, I think you do,' he said softly. 'It's just the method of payment we're arguing about, isn't it—not the necessity for it?'

He move away from the bed and opened the armoire, tossing several prettily wrapped packages on to her bed.

'Try pretending it's Christmas,' he told her flippantly. 'When I was doing this I didn't know whether to buy things for the girl you were or the woman you should have become.'

'And which did you decide on?'

'Look for yourself,' he suggested.

'I'm not going to wear them!'

'Not willingly perhaps,' he agreed, 'but wear them you will—understand that, Laurel. You've clung to the past for too long. It's over—finished.'

'It can never be over,' she told him fiercely, 'can't you understand that? Can't you see that every time a man looks at me or touches me. . . .'

'He becomes your stepfather? Of course I can see it, Laurel. But the issues aren't as clear-cut as that, are they?' he suggested, watching her.

'I don't know what you mean.'

'No? I think you do. You hate me nearly as much as you hate him. He's gone beyond your reach, but I'm still here. Sometimes the only way to stop a forest fire is to start another, do you understand what I'm trying to tell you?'

'No,' she told him shortly, appalled by his astuteness.

'I think you do, but never mind, one step at a time will do me fine for now. So, are you going to open those parcels and thank me nicely, or would you prefer me to drag you screaming from that bed and put them on you?'

Strangely enough she was not frightened of him

sexually; her rage against him was too great for that, and with fingers that trembled uncontrollably she unwrapped the gaily wrapped packages.

One contained a minute bikini in autumn gold and sizzling blue, so brief that she couldn't imagine herself wearing it. To her chagrin Oliver laughed at the expression on her face.

'Quite modest by South of France standards, I can assure you,' he told her. 'Madame in the boutique would much have preferred to sell me a sexy cache-sex, consisting of little more than a minute triangle of silk and a pretty ribbon. Normally I'm not an advocate of any female apart from the adolescent going topless, but in your case. . . .' His eyes returned thoughtfully to her breasts, causing her to shrink deeper into the bed.

'Open the rest of them,' Oliver instructed, throwing them towards her. 'The bikini you can wear when you're sunbathing, but even I have to admit it isn't quite the thing for taking dictation in.'

One of the other parcels contained emerald cut-off jeans and a brief white tee-shirt, plain but very obviously expensive, another a cream linen skirt, with a toning striped blazer and a brilliant peacock blue blouse. There was a button-through cotton dress, two pairs of shoes, and then in the last parcel several sets of underwear; all plain white; all beautifully made in satin and lace.

'Bra and briefs only,' Oliver told her dryly. 'Something tells me you've a long way to go before you start choosing underwear with a lover in mind rather than simple necessity.'

'I'll never do that,' Laurel told him jerkily, flinging the garments away as though they had contaminated her. 'I'd rather die than wear anything you bought for me!' What was the matter with her? For a moment she had almost felt tears pricking her eyes.

'Ah, but then there are fates far worse than death, aren't there, Laurel?' he reminded her cruelly. 'Try telling yourself it's like taking nasty medicine and that it's good for you in the long run. Can you honestly tell me you don't want to be able to give and receive love, Laurel?'

The angry words she wanted to utter died on her lips at the image he had conjured up. A bitter yearning filled her, and she was acutely aware of a sensation of terrible loss. She couldn't afford to give way to such weaknesses. Ruthlessly she reminded herself why she had come to France.

'Get dressed,' Oliver told her, scooping up her hairclips from the dresser where she had left them. 'Leave your hair down. Be brave, Laurel, take the first step back into life. You can do it, you know.'

After he had gone she did contemplate simply remaining where she was, but she knew that he would simply return and do as he had threatened— dress her himself. A wave of sheer resentment flooded over her. How dared he take over her life in this high-handed manner? But it wouldn't be for long, she comforted herself. She would soon find some means of turning the tables on him. There must be something she could discover about him that she could use to her own advantage. All she had to do was to discover it!

She dressed in one of the silky bras he had bought for her, flushing as she realised how accurately he had guessed her measurements. The soft fabric clung seductively to her curves, making her aware of her femininity; the matching briefs were tiny and she hastily averted her eyes from her body, wondering a little at the heat that suddenly overwhelmed her.

She chose to wear the cut-off jeans and the tee-shirt, feeling strange having her hair curling down past her shoulders instead of restricted on top of her head.

'Very good,' Oliver pronounced when she finally plucked up the courage to go downstairs. 'Now you look like a girl of twenty-two.' He reached up, brushing his knuckles against her skin before she could move away.

'Real peaches and cream,' he stated softly, 'and eyelashes so dark they don't need mascara. You're a very attractive lady, Laurel.'

'You don't have to pay me compliments,' she told him in a stilted voice, 'especially as we both know they aren't true.'

'No?' His eyebrows rose.' And just what the hell do you know about the truth? All you know is what your stepfather told you, isn't it Laurel? Didn't he tell you, you were desirable?'

Panic clawed at her stomach, horror screaming through her veins. She wanted to turn and run; blot out his question; anything to hide from the memories it evoked. His glance seared her with its fierce intensity.

'Didn't he, Laurel?' Oliver pressed, grasping her arm as though he sensed her desire to flee.

'You know what he told me,' she said bitterly. 'You wrote it all down . . . he told me I led him on, he. . . .'

'He told you you were desirable,' Oliver repeated inexorably. 'He told you that, didn't he, Laurel, didn't he?'

'Yes, yes. . . .' Suddenly she was screaming the word. Her hands pressed over the ears to obliterate his tormenting questions. Tears spurted from her eyes and she was seized in a vortex of pain and anguish, barely aware of Oliver's arms coming round her, cradling her while she sobbed convulsively against his shoulder. As she got her emotions back under control, she became aware of the fact that she was in Oliver's arms; that he was stroking her hair, soothing her with soft whispers, gentling her, she realised with a stab of perception, as though she were a terrified wild creature.

'That's nothing to be ashamed of in having someone desire you, Laurel.' he told her quietly. 'No blame attached to it. He was a sick man— mentally sick—Good heavens, if I'd....' He broke off, his mouth hard and compressed.

'He said I led him on. He made my mother believe it. You believed it; everyone believed it....'

'And you believed it,' he guessed, lifting her chin with his thumbs and forcing her to meet his eyes, his earlier anger replaced by compassion, but strangely, for once it did not anger her. Instead she felt curiously weak.

'No.... Yes.... I....'

She pulled away from him, still dazed by the emotional storm his questions had evoked. No one had ever got to her like that—not in six years. She started to shake with reaction and made no demur as he pushed her down into a chair and poured her a cup of coffee, practicality replacing compassion.

'It's bound to be traumatic,' he told her. 'But you will fly free, Laurel.' And from the way he said it she couldn't tell if it was a promise or a threat. Had he guessed that sometimes in those awful nightmares that seized her, he was the one bending over her, pinning her to the floor, touching her.... Perspiration broke out on her forehead, and she pushed her cup away, knowing that she was going to be sick, if she so much as took a sip of it, all thoughts of revenge forgotten in the wave of emotion engulfing her.

'Like I already said, I've some reading to catch up on, so try taking it easy for today.'

'So you can try a different experiment on me tomorrow?' she asked bitterly. 'Do you really think wearing different clothes is going to make me into a different person?' She had to whip up her anger against him, she had to!

'I don't think so, but obviously you do, otherwise you wouldn't have chosen to wear the ones you did before, would you?' he pointed out with a logic she couldn't refute. 'If it helps try telling yourself that fate has brought us together again, Laurel, giving us both a chance to escape from the past. I know you don't want to, but you must learn to talk about what happened. You're carrying a terrible burden of self-blame and guilt, and there's no need. You have nothing to blame yourself for, or to feel guilty about. Unlike. . . .' He broke off as she saw the expression of disbelief in her eyes.

'Is it so impossible to believe that I might feel guilty?' he asked harshly. 'My word, Laurel, do you think me so devoid of human feelings? Do you really see me as such a monster?'

She started to tremble, reacting against her will to the taut emotion of his voice, at first barely paying attention as he continued to talk to her, slowly becoming aware of how skilfully he was drawing her out, of how much she had already confided to him as she responded to his careful probing.

'Laurel, don't you see?' he demanded when she suddenly clammed up. 'If we talk it through it. . . .'

'Will ease your guilt?' she supplied scornfully. 'I don't. . . .'

'Believe me?' For a moment she could almost have believed she saw pain and remorse mingling in his eyes, but the expression was gone so quickly she couldn't really analyse it. 'Strange though it may seem to you I don't exactly relish the thought of what I've done to you—not singlehandedly perhaps, but I certainly did my bit to contribute. Is it too late for me to make amends?'

Did he really think she would give her trust to him so easily a second time? Laurel asked herself bitterly, forcing herself to ignore the tug of response his words evoked. He had been using her then and now. And now she was determined to use him—but how? Suddenly she had the germ of an idea.

On his own admission he had been wrong about her; how many more of those, clever, acclaimed articles of his had been based on biased opinion rather than hard fact? Perhaps none, but if there was only one . . . that would be enough to discredit him as a reporter, and if she could discredit him as the reporter he had once been, she could discredit him as the writer he now was. Ignoring the thrust of distaste she couldn't quite smother, she pursued the idea. What she needed were copies of all his old articles so that she could study them. Was he likely to have any here at the farmhouse?

He was talking to her again, this time about the court case, and she stilled the pain starting deep down inside her, forcing herself to try to answer his questions; perhaps she might be able to ask some of her own if she managed to get him off guard enough.

'Trust me, Laurel,' he urged her. 'It's a big step for you to take, I know, but. . . .'

'You want to help me?'

'Someone some time has to break through the

wall you've built around yourself. The last time we met you were still a child ... now you're a woman. In the eyes of the world that is; in your own eyes you're still very much a frightened child.'

He was perceptive; too perceptive. Fear lanced through her, darkening her eyes, her faint gasp of pain bringing his attention to her face.

'Laurel!'

She must be going mad, she thought numbly, because for one crazy moment she had almost believed she saw anguish in his eyes and heard a raw bitterness in the way he grated her name. But that was impossible.

'I want to help you,' he reiterated softly. 'Are you prepared to meet me halfway; to make an effort to rejoin the human race? Have you got the guts?'

It seemed impossible that he couldn't sense her hostility towards him; she was so afraid she might betray it, but it was essential that she get under his guard. Her pride objected furiously to the tiny inner voice warning her to caution. She wanted to fling his offer of 'help' back in his face, but if she did that she would lose whatever chance she might have of discrediting him.

'I ... I don't know,' she managed huskily at last. 'But I'll try.'

'You won't be sorry,' he promised softly, and then incredibly his lips brushed hers lightly and were gone before she could protest, her fingers going involuntarily to the quivering softness of her mouth, her eyes mirroring her disbelief. Just for a moment she had felt the strangest emotion; a mixture of excitement and dread; a weird sensation unlike any other she had known.

Deep down inside her warning bells started to clamour, where there was emotion there was danger.

'I'll be working in the living room if you want me for anything,' Oliver told her, breaking into her thoughts. 'Why don't you go out for a walk—familiarise yourself with the place, but don't wander too far, it's only May, I know, but that sun out there is hot.'

'Yes, I think I will.' Laurel turned towards the door, too engrossed in her own thoughts to notice the look he gave her, until he said softly, 'Laurel?'

Her head jerked up their eyes meeting. Laurel felt for some reason as though she were poised on the edge of an abyss, teetering dangerously there, and that somehow Oliver had the power to either drag her over or leave her safely where she was. He moved toward her, checking suddenly.

'I like the outfit,' he told her slowly, and for some reason, when he turned away it was dissatisfaction that niggled away at her rather than relief.

Outside the sun was hot, as he had warned her. A little to her surprise she discovered an elegant paved patio at the rear of the house, decorated with stone tubs, but it had become neglected and weeds were beginning to creep between the stones. Laurel followed the path that led down to the olive grove and found the swimming pool, now half filled with water.

It didn't look as garish as she had visualised and was surprisingly large, protected from any breeze by a hedge of cypresses. There were changing rooms and a barbecue pit, but Laurel only gave these a brief investigation before returning to the house. As she crossed the neglected patio something made her stop and kneel down to tug gently at some of the weeds. Once begun, the task engrossed her and she worked on heedless of time or effort, finding a growing satisfaction in the pile of weeds at her side and the neatness of the paving when they were removed. Alone, with the sun warming her back and faint birdsong the only sound to disturb the peace, it was easier to clarify her thoughts and intentions. She had asked for this job because she wanted to punish Oliver for what he had done to her, but somehow he had turned the tables on her and was going to use her presence for his own ends—but what were they? Turning her into a woman, was what he had said, but what exactly did that involve? she wondered with misgiving. Already he had proved that she was no match for him when it came to a direct clash of wills. Witness this morning, and the clothes he had made her wear. Laurel sat up, frowning. It was odd that after six years of dressing as she had and wearing her hair screwed up so tightly that not a single curl could escape, today she had worn casual clothes and let her hair down for the first time, and yet working here on the patio she had completely forgotten about it. It had taken the momentary sight of her own reflection to remind her that the girl in the cut-off jeans and long flowing hair was her!

When the psychiatrist had first come to see her at the home, he had told her that one day, when she was ready, she would want to break through the wall she had built round herself; he had also suggested that she might find it helpful to write down her thoughts and feelings; to keep a diary, in effect, but Laurel had rejected the idea outright. Her thoughts were so tortured that she couldn't even bear to do that. And yet now.... Disposing of the weeds, she hurried inside, listening for a moment at the living-room door.

Apart from the occasional rustle of paper all was quiet, which meant, she guessed shrewdly, that

Oliver didn't want to be disturbed. Well, that suited her.

She went upstairs, washed her hands, and stared assessingly for a few minutes at her reflection. Surely her cheekbones had not always been so clearly defined, her eyes so large and sparkling? Even her mouth seemed different somehow, softer, more sensual, she recognised on a shock-wave of distaste.

In her room she removed the notepad she always carried in her bag and, seated by the window, began to write, slowly at first and then more quickly as the thoughts flowed. She started with the sudden re-emergence of Oliver into her life, trying to clarify her thoughts and emotions, writing a little unevenly as she admitted her desire for revenge; the sudden painful burgeoning of the first real emotion she had felt for six years.

When at last she laid aside her pencil she was frowning thoughtfully. It was strange; in some ways she felt more at home; more right as the girl she now was and had been for only a brief span of hours—and yet how could that be when Oliver had forced that girl upon her?

As she sat there it occurred to her that ever since they had met again Oliver had set out quite deliberately to provoke her into anger, alternating this treatment with a compassion that occasionally verged on the paternal. She wasn't a fool, there had to be some ulterior motive for his behaviour. She might not know what it was yet, but at least, knowing helped to strengthen her resolve to be on her guard, reminded her that she was here for one purpose and one alone, and it had nothing to do with Oliver's 'experiment', as she termed his behaviour towards her. She didn't believe for one moment that his motives were as altrusitic as he had told her; she couldn't believe it, not after what he had written about her. Of course he had explained that away very neatly, but how did she know it was true? How did she know he wasn't simply planning a follow-up story or a full-length novel?—it would make riveting reading done in the inimitable Jonathan Graves style.

Oliver emerged from the living room for a salad lunch which Laurel had made. She had discovered a small kitchen garden, and Oliver told her that he had employed someone to take care of the gardens, but that he had died quite recently and that was why they were so neglected.

'I could do a little bit while we're here,' she offered, surprising a sharp glance from him.

'You like gardening?'

'It can be therapeutic,' she told him evasively, 'and besides. . . .'

'It's a means of keeping away from me?' he supplied. 'Well, whatever turns you on, but you're employed here primarily as a secretary, remember, Laurel, not a gardener, and I wouldn't advise too much exposure to the sun until you become a little more acclimatised. You were out there long enough this morning for one day.'

'You were watching me?' She found it disconcerting to realise that he had seen her; watched her while she hadn't known he was there.

'Is it a crime?' he asked her ironically. 'Yes, I was watching you, and you looked like a little girl totally absorbed in some adult task.' He got up swiftly and walked towards her, bending over her so that her breath became constricted in her throat. 'Next time you go out, wear a hat,' he told her, sliding his fingers into her hair and lifting the weight of it from her neck. 'Lovely though this is, it's no protection from the sun.'

And then to her consternation he lifted a handful of her hair and breathed in the scent of it before letting it run fluidly through his fingers. Lightning seemed to run along her nerve ends at his touch.

'It smells of sunshine and thyme, and freedom, Laurel, a more erotic combination than the most expensive perfume in the world.' And then with the abrupt changes of front she was becoming accustomed to he said coolly. 'I still have one hell of a lot to get through. I'll have my coffee in the living room. Will you object if I leave the evening meal to you tonight? With a bit of luck I might manage to get a swim in before dusk and then tomorrow we'll start work proper.' He sounded almost curt, his expression grimly withdrawn—more so than his words occasioned.

Later, alone with her book, Laurel found herself touching the silken strands of her hair with nervous fingers, remembering how he had touched it. Why did he do things like that? Was he constantly trying to unnerve her? What reaction did he want from her? Terror? She frowned and picked up her notebook, reading through what she had written that morning.

It was a revelation to discover that despite her hatred of Oliver, what she had written betrayed none of the restraint or fear she had experienced with other men. He had angered her, yes; and there had been fear when he touched her, but it was not fear of him. The mere fact that he knew about her past seemed to make a subtle link between them which she could not break; it was as though because he knew of her fear and the reason for it, she didn't need the protective barrier of it. In some strange way the fact that he did know was almost a relief, freeing her from the need to

pretend. . . . She caught herself up. Pretend what?
That she found men and sex abhorrent? That was
no pretence. It was real—real! Throwing the
notebook on one side, she went downstairs,
busying herself with the preparation of the evening
meal, forbidding herself to let her thoughts roam
as they had done in her room. What was the
matter with her? Why all these inward heart-
searchings? What was happening to her?

Because they had only had a light lunch Laurel
decided to make a chicken casserole for their
evening meal. Cookery was one of her hobbies,
and it didn't take long to find enough in the
garden and freezer to have the makings of a
savoury concoction.

The smell of it had begun to permeate the whole
kitchen when Oliver walked in, the dark hair
ruffled as though impatient fingers had been
dragged through it, a strained look in his eyes.

'I need some fresh air,' he told Laurel.
'Something smells good—how long will it be?

'It's chicken casserole, and it will be another
hour or so yet.'

'Good,' he announced equably, 'then you've got
no excuse for refusing to come down to the pool
with me.'

'None at all, apart from the fact that I can't
swim,' she agreed coolly. 'Anyway, I do have
something of my own to do.'

'You do?' He frowned and Laurel wished she
had said nothing. What if he were to ask her what
she was doing? It occurred to her that his absence
from the house would give her an opportunity to
search for copies of his early articles, but
something within her shrank from going through
someone else's personal belongings.

'Something tells me you're beginning to forget what you're doing down here, Laurel,' he told her in an ominously hard voice. 'You're here as my employee, and if I say you're coming down to the pool with me that's exactly what you're going to do. I'll see you down there in exactly ten minutes,' he told her, not giving her the opportunity to argue, as he opened the door, pausing by it for a couple of seconds as he added with iron inflexibility, 'Oh, and Laurel—put the bikini on!'

This time he didn't add the threat that if she didn't, he would, but it was there, unspoken between them.

She followed him upstairs slowly, when she judged she had left sufficient time for him to reach his room. What was she so afraid of? she asked herself as she went upstairs; why did she feel this acute sense of terror? Hadn't she just been congratulating herself on the fact that she wasn't afraid of him, and now suddenly. . . .

As she stripped off her jeans and blouse her eyes were glued on her bedroom door, as though she expected with every second that passed that Oliver intended to come in—just as in the old days her stepfather had done before she bought that lock. She tensed as she heard his door open and close and his progress along the landing, past her room, and she was drowning in a sea of fear, trembling with it, unable to understand why she had ever agreed to come here alone with this man—with any man. And then he was gone, walking down the stairs, and her terror lifted slowly, her body starting to relax. She stared at herself in the mirror. She had lost all the warm colour she had gained out in the garden. Her eyes looked huge and bruised somehow. She simply couldn't go out there now. But she knew she had to, otherwise

Oliver would come back and he would make her and there would be no compassion, no escape. It was really the lesser of two evils, she acknowledged as she slid out of her bra and briefs and into the bikini. There was a brief robe to go with it, and she snatched it up from the bed, startled by the sudden reflection of her body in the cheval mirror. Unwillingly she stared at her body—something she had always avoided doing since her teens. It was like looking at a stranger; a shockingly feminine stranger whose curves seemed made for the brief scraps of silk, and whose skin glowed with a soft sheen, even though it was pale and untouched by the sun. She couldn't go outside dressed like this, she thought, aghast. She might just as well walk out there nude. . . . But other girls did it, she reminded herself; she had seen photographs in glossy holiday brochures; in magazines. From the past Rachel's voice came back to her. 'Never be ashamed of your body, Laurel,' she had told her. 'It's very beautiful. It's only your stepfather's thoughts that make you think it's ugly.'

Was she beautiful? Would Oliver think she was? Why had she thought that? Why had she thought of Oliver at all? Because he was the one to force her into this situation? Did he know that she was cowering up here afraid of him seeing her like this? And yet hadn't she admitted only this morning that she wasn't afraid of him—at least, not in the way she had feared her stepfather?

If she didn't go downstairs, he would only come and drag her out, she reflected uneasily as she pulled on the brief silk robe and tied the belt. Whoever heard of a silk bikini and wrap? It was so impracticable. Impracticable but beautiful, an inner voice contradicted. The silk caressed her skin softly, and with a jolting shock she realised she enjoyed the sensation of the fabric against her. It was like ... like. ... Her face burned suddenly as she realised the only thing she could compare the sensation with was the touch of Oliver's hands on her skin. But she hadn't liked that. She had hated it, just as she hated him.

He was already lying beside the pool when she walked hesitantly towards it. He had his back towards her, but he rolled over as though he had heard her coming, surveying her from eyes shielded from the sun by his hand.

He was wearing brief black trunks, so brief that after one shocked look Laurel averted her eyes from the tanned flesh of his body, almost stumbling along the path.

'I was just about to come and get you,' he told her lazily, apparently unaware of her embarrassment. 'Come and lie down here.' He patted a sun-lounger drawn up next to his own, smiling a little sardonically as Laurel skirted behind him to reach it.

'Did you bring some protective cream with you?' he demanded as she perched awkwardly on the lounger, her back hunched protectively. 'The sun is still pretty powerful, but at a guess I would say your skin isn't the type to burn, is it?'

'I. ...' How could she tell him that she didn't know? That she had never sunbathed as other girls did, and that right now her stomach was heaving protestingly at the thought that all she was wearing was several brief scraps of silk, a very perilous defence against the eyes of such men as her stepfather.

'There's no need to cling on to that thing as though it's a life-raft, Laurel,' Oliver told her sardonically, suddenly moving so that he too was sitting up, and although she still had her back to him, out of the corner of her eye she could see his feet placed firmly on the tiles and she knew that the slightest movement would bring the bare sun-tanned length of his thigh against hers.

She tensed as she waited for him to demand that she remove her robe, and was surprised to discover within herself a sense of anti-climax when he said instead,

'Now that you're here you can oil my back for me. Unlike you I've no desire to burn. A real martyr, aren't you, Laurel?' he goaded softly, 'And like all martyrs you enjoy the thought of burning for your sins; isn't that right?'

'I don't know what you mean,' she told him stiffly, taking the bottle of oil he handed her, and glad that he had turned on to his stomach so that he couldn't see the dark colour running up under her skin. She did know what he meant, or what she thought he meant. He was trying to suggest that she enjoyed being frigid and unresponsive to men; that it was a form of self-punishment, but that wasn't true? Was it?

'Do my shoulders first, will you?'

The lazy command focused her attention on the breadth of his torso, her eyes drifting in helpless fascination down the length of his spine and the masculinity of his hips. His legs were long, sprinkled with dark hairs, and at the thought of touching them a thousand nerves jumped in protest under her skin.

'What's the matter, Laurel?' Just in time she caught the note of hard anger in his voice. 'Have I got to remind you again that I'm not your stepfather? I'm just a man like any other, and by no stretch of the imagination am I so starved of sex that I'm about to pounce on you the moment you touch me!'

He turned and looked mockingly at her over his shoulder, his eyes suddenly narrowing intently. She looked down and realised that her robe had come open.

'And take that damned thing off,' he growled, 'otherwise I might start thinking you're wearing it because you want me to take it off for you!'

As he turned away to rest his forehead on his forearms, and was taking absolutely no notice of her at all, Laurel couldn't see the point in refusing. And besides, if she did, he might actually think she did want him to ... to.... Hurriedly shrugging off the robe, she folded it neatly and placed it on her lounger, only realising as she lent to retrieve that bottle of oil that Oliver had rolled over on to his back and was watching her with a strange expression in his eyes, a small smile playing at the corners of his mouth.

'So that's the way to do it,' he marvelled. 'If you want to get a girl out of her clothes, promise to do it for her. Well, well—and to think all these years I actually thought they preferred it the other way round!'

He had tricked her, she thought angrily, unaware that her emotions were registering in the darkening of her eyes and the tensing of her muscles. She had thought he wasn't going to look at her, and now.... She had a sudden overwhelming longing to run away and hide herself from him, and she couldn't bear the way his eyes drifted slowly over her body. She remembered how her stepfather had looked at her; how greedily his eyes had roamed her body. She tensed, and Oliver rolled over again, closing his eyes as he murmured,

'Very nice. Your skin is still a little pale, of course, but you're as nicely put together as any other girl your age. Now do my back for me, will you, there's a good girl.'

Again she experienced a let-down feeling; was that what was called damning with faint praise? she wondered absently as she unscrewed the lotion and knelt down beside him. What had she expected? He wasn't her stepfather, he kept on telling her so; he was an experienced male who doubtless found her repression amusing. It was obvious from the way he lay perfectly relaxed and at ease that she had absolutely no effect upon him at all. Which was exactly what she wanted, wasn't it?

She was so engrossed in her task that it was several seconds before her fingers relayed to her brain the message that there was a distinct and almost shocking pleasure to be found in touching a man's skin. Oliver's felt warm from the sun, and oddly soft unlike the muscles beneath it. She touched tentative fingers to his spine, idly tracing the line of it, coming to an abrupt stop as he drawled mockingly, 'You're supposed to be oiling my skin, not giving yourself a lesson in anatomy!' He sounded grimly angry, and she stared numbly at him.

'I. . . .'

'You what?' Was it her imagination or had he paled slightly under his tan? 'Got carried away? Surely not, Laurel? It seems to me that when you accuse me of indulging in experiments, you might be guilty of trying a few yourself. Go ahead, but don't be surprised if I start wanting to try out a few of my own.' He half turned and looked at her puzzled, hesitant eyes. 'What you were just doing arouses some highly erotic sensations, Laurel,' he told her sardonically, 'You don't believe me? Then perhaps I'd better just show you.'

Before she could guess what was going to happen he had tugged her down beside him. The lounger was only narrow, and even lying on her side, it was impossible to avoid coming into contact with his body. One arm circled her waist, the other propping up his head as he looked into her dazed and disbelieving eyes. His own were dark, glittering faintly as they studied her.

'No. . . .' she whispered jerkily, moistening dry lips. 'No, Oliver, I. . . .'

'You're a great one for saying no, before you know what you're refusing, aren't you?' he mocked, calmly ignoring her. 'I'm not going to hurt you, Laurel. Just keep still.'

Whatever it was she had glimpsed in his eyes a moment earlier had gone and they were once again calm and assessing, and yet she had the distinct impression that he was exerting stringent control over his real feelings, masking them with an assumed calmness.

'Lie still!' he reiterated softly.

CHAPTER SIX

SHE was far too terrified to do anything else, and yet as the seconds ticked by and Oliver did no more than calmly smooth the oil into her neck and shoulders she found her body relaxing into the rhythmic movements of his hand. In fact it was so pleasantly soothing that she felt her eyes beginning to close, a deliciously warm, languorous sensation spreading through her body. If she was a cat she would be purring, she thought drowsily, opening her eyes to find Oliver watching her with an unreadable expression in his eyes.

'That,' he told her, 'is someone oiling your back, but this. . . .' Without any warning his hand left her shoulder, stroking slowly downwards over her spine, mirroring, she realised with a stab of startled dismay, the way she had touched him. Various emotions chased each other over her face as his thumb made circular patterns on her spine and curious sensations spiralled along it. Had he really felt like this when she touched him?

When she lifted bemused brown eyes to comprehending grey ones he murmured softly, 'You see?—quite, quite different isn't it?'

'I. . . .'

'Shush!'

The arm curved round her waist was suddenly removed, and she was lying on her back, with Oliver leaning over her. She tried to move and his fingers gripped her shoulder pinning her down, trapping her. . . . A panicky scream filled her throat, terror a black nightmare sea in which she was totally submerged, a dull roaring blackness devouring her.

The darkness cleared and she heard Oliver calling her name quietly. She opened her eyes. She was still lying on the lounger, but now he was crouching beside her, making no attempt to touch her.

'All right now?'

'I. . . .'

'You fainted,' he told her brusquely.' He glanced up at the sky. 'It's getting cooler, we might as well go in. You go ahead. I'll follow you when I've cleared this lot away. Here, don't forget this,' he warned, handing her her wrap. And as she walked towards the farmhouse, Laurel had the distinct impression that beneath his outward calm he was a man in the grip of a raging anger. Because she had fainted? Because his experiment failed? She shivered suddenly, and it wasn't simply because of the evening breeze. What had she done, agreeing to come down here? Why did he want her here?

It was a thought that hammered at her brain both that night and in the days that followed, although Oliver didn't give her much time for daydreaming.

Once he started work, she was astounded at his output; already in three days the first chapter was almost finished. It was hard to judge the line of the story from it because the initial pages dealt mainly with the primary character, a man tortured by a sense of guilt for a past crime of which the reader was as yet unaware, and yet as she typed the dictation he had given her, Laurel found herself sympathising with the man; he stirred an elusive chord of memory within her; something that glimmered in and out of her subconscious mind but would not allow itself to be grasped.

Oliver had become almost withdrawn, barely communicative even at meal times, and she had almost forgotten the incident by the pool. Almost, but not quite. Sometimes at night, when she couldn't sleep she remembered the feel of his skin beneath her fingers; the emotions he had aroused in her when he touched her; had *he* felt like that when she touched him? the thought was shockingly exciting, and strange sensations coiled through her stomach.

Every morning while Oliver worked on his notes she spent half an hour or so in the garden. She enjoyed her self-imposed task, and found that it helped to clarify her thoughts. She was still writing in her notebook, still trying to find ways and means of accomplishing her revenge. As yet she had not been able to bring herself to search through the bookshelves looking for something that might help her, but Oliver was reticent about his past life, and she knew she would never have the courage to question him directly.

Her need to be revenged upon him was constantly warring with her conscience; but stubbornly she refused to listen to it, quelling all her doubts.

One particularly hot afternoon when Oliver had told her he didn't need her any more that day, as he wanted to do some thinking, Laurel abandoned the garden in favour of the pool. She hadn't returned there since that first time, but strangely today, for some reason she felt an urge to lie in the sun and feel its warmth beating into her flesh.

This time she didn't feel quite as exposed in the brief bikini, but she still wore the wrap.

The poolside was deserted as she expected and she dragged one of the loungers into the sun and spread a towel on it, smoothing cream into her skin so that she wouldn't burn.

The sun was deliciously warm, the brilliant light bouncing off the water causing her to close her eyes. When she did so, she could almost imagine that the heat of the sun copied the warmth of Oliver's hands, and a tiny tremor feathered along her spine, her stomach muscles tensing protestingly at her wayward thoughts.

The heat of the sun made her drowsy and as she drifted off to sleep she wondered a little how much she had changed since coming to Provence; since meeting Oliver, really. Now she thought nothing of leaving her hair loose about her face; about wearing the clothes he had bought her, about. . . .

She opened her eyes, sensing that she was no longer alone. Oliver stood there, looking grim.

She scrambled up, dislodging one of her bikini straps as she did so.

'Didn't you hear me calling you?'

'I was asleep,' she told him muzzily. 'I didn't think you'd want me. You said I could have the rest of the afternoon to myself.'

'But I didn't think you'd be stupid enough to lie out here and burn.' He knelt down beside her, touching her shoulder, and she winced, realising that he was right and she had burned a little, but that seemed scant reason for the anger she could sense rigidly banked down inside him.

'I had no idea you were here,' he told her. 'I thought you were in the garden. I thought you'd gone,' he said roughly.

'Gone?'

What on earth could he mean? Where could she have gone?

'Yes, gone, left, run away,' he elucidated, plainly on the verge of losing his temper, 'but no, I find you're here, blithely sunbathing, oblivious to the fact that. . . .' He brought himself up sharply, clamping down on whatever it was he was going to say, and Laurel was glad. His anger frightened her.

'It was so nice I thought I'd sunbathe,' she said lamely.

'So I see.'

He seemed to be back to his normal sardonic self, and she breathed a faint sigh of relief.

'You're going to have strap marks,' he told her, bending down to tug her strap back into place. The cooling contact of his fingers against her skin produced a strange little frisson of pleasure, so unexpected that she stiffened.

'Oh, for Pete's sake!' he practically snarled. 'I'm not about to rape you, Laurel. I thought we'd established that fact, although heaven knows, the way you act is enough to drive a man to it. I. . . .'

Laurel wasn't listening. He had just echoed her stepfather's accusations; he had said that too. He had said she asked for it, and that was what Oliver was saying. She got up blindly, oblivious to Oliver's presence, to everything but the words hammering inside her head, walking and then running blindly in her attempt to escape from them. She heard Oliver call out something she couldn't catch, and then suddenly she was plunging into the pool, the water an icy shock against her overheated skin. She tried to breathe, gulping a mouthful of water, choking in her panic as she tried to find the bottom with her feet, fighting for breath as she struggled beneath the surface, ears, eyes, nose and throat all clogged with the life-depriving water.

Someone was tugging at her hands, trying to stop her breathing, dragging her beneath the surface. She tore at the fingers grasping her arms, then panic exploded inside her as she fell into a whirlpool of darkness.

Someone was breathing erratically beside her, hurting her chest, forcing her to breathe. She tried to protest and instead was humiliatingly sick.

She gave a weak cough and a spluttering breath, then opened her eyes to discover that she was lying by the pool and that Oliver was standing over her, his jeans and shirt soaked, water dripping off his clothes and body.

'Next time you decide to try and walk on water, give me some warning, will you?' he demanded grittily, adding, 'What the hell were you trying to do, Laurel? Drown yourself because I touched you?'

Not because you touched me, she wanted to say, and not drown myself even; it was just what you said ... what you said ... what my stepfather said, the words whirled through her mind, but her throat was too sore for her to utter them. She started to shiver with reaction, making no protest when Oliver bent and scooped her up in his arms. His shirt was plastered to his skin and she could feel the heat coming off it burning into her cold body.

As he carried her towards the house she realised hazily that being held in his arms wasn't unpleasant. On the contrary, she felt ... safe.

'Starting from tomorrow, you're going to learn to swim,' she heard him say as she carried her upstairs. 'You can make a martyr out of yourself, but you're not going to make one out of me,' he told her obliquely. 'I've already got enough crosses to bear.'

He carried her into her bedroom and dropped her on the bed. 'Don't move,' he warned her. 'You're still in shock. Don't worry if you feel like being sick. You swallowed one hell of a lot of water.'

'Where are you going?' Laurel watched him from the bed, eyes round and uncertain, not wanting him to go and yet unable to ask him to stay.

'To run you a bath,' he told her shortly. 'You're frozen, and like I said, still in shock.' When he had gone she closed her eyes, mutely accepting what he had said; it was too much of an effort to do anything else. A bath, he had said, and the thought of warm water against her skin was distinctly appealing.

She was drifting off on a hazy cloud when he returned. He had changed into a towelling robe, belted round the waist, but for once she felt no shock or curl of nervous excitement at the sight of his body, merely an apathetic acceptance of his presence and her need of it.

'Laurel.'

She wanted to tell him that she wanted to sleep, but he wouldn't let her. He picked her up, shaking her so hard that she was forced to open her eyes. His were black with anger, so much anger that the haze started to clear.

'Don't go passing out on me again,' he warned her as he made her walk across the landing and into the bathroom.

'Get in,' he instructed, testing the water, 'and no, I'm not going. It's as easy to drown in a bath as it is in a pool when you're on the verge of losing consciousness.'

For some strange reason she felt merely apathetic acceptance of his commands. She even stayed listlessly passive as he removed her bikini, shivering slightly with cold, goosebumps raised on her skin.

'Laurel.' There was a curious tightness in the way he said her name; an inflection she couldn't understand, and which quickly changed to anger when she tried to focus on him.

'Oh, for Pete's sake,' she heard him mutter under his breath as he bundled her into the water, and its life-giving warmth started to melt the frozen ice in her veins.

She could have stayed there all night, but Oliver seemed to have other ideas. He whisked her out before she could protest, enveloping her in a huge towel and briskly towelling her body, until her skin stung with pain.

'That's better,' he drawled acidly, as she cried out in protest. 'That's more like the Laurel I know and. . . .'

'Hate,' she supplied for him through chattering teeth.

'Stay here,' he told her, 'and I'll go downstairs and get you some brandy. What on earth possessed you?' he added, watching her with anger darkened eyes. 'Was drowning really preferable to being touched by me?'

'It wasn't that. It was what you said,' she admitted, too shaken to care about what she might be revealing.

'What did I say?' he probed, wrapping her in a thick bathrobe which she idly recognised as one of his.

'You said I could drive a man to rape.'

'And because of that you fling yourself headfirst into the pool?'

'It was what he said,' she told him in a low voice. 'My stepfather. He said it was my fault, and that—that. . . .' She couldn't go on. Her throat was tense with anguished pain. Oliver had been rubbing her hair dry, but he released the towel and stepped back as though she were made from the most brittle china, a tiny muscle pulsing under his skin, the lean jaw taut.

'Oh dear, Laurel, and ·you thought. ... Oh, Laurel, I.... Stay here,' he told her huskily. 'I won't be long.'

Now he was being kind to her again, she thought dispassionately. He was always kind to her after he had been particularly hurtful. It was all part of his experiment, of course, but somehow she hadn't got the energy to care. All she wanted to do was curl up in his arms and. ... She stiffened as she realised the direction of her thoughts. She wanted to be in Oliver's arms! But. ...

Before she could delve any deeper into her feelings he was back, his expression grimly withdrawn, a small glass of dark amber liquid in one hand.

'Drink this,' he told her expressionlessly, 'and then I'd better do something about those shoulders, otherwise you won't be able to move in the morning.'

The brandy burned its way down her throat, inducing a delicious warmth in her stomach and a heady sensation that suddenly seemed to free her from all the restrictions she had always placed on herself. She slid her arms round Oliver's neck when he picked her up, smiling at him when he tensed and looked down into her face.

'Dutch courage, little girl,' he told her sardonically, 'but don't press your luck too far—I *am* only flesh and blood, remember!'

And she was still trying to decipher that remark when he placed her on her bed.

'Where's your nightdress?' he asked her shortly, as she lay watching him. She told him and he got. it, grimacing as he saw the voluminous folds of cotton and the prim high-buttoned neck. 'You can't wear this,' he told her curtly, 'the cotton will rub those shoulders raw. Have you nothing else?'

She shook her haad, amazed that she should feel so little embarrassment.

'Well, I'm afraid I have nothing you can borrow. The only thing I like against my skin in bed is . . . skin,' he told her lightly. 'You should try it some time.'

'Perhaps I will.'

He couldn't have looked more astounded if she'd hurled a bomb at him. Giggles welled up inside her, tickling her throat. All at once she felt totally carefree and uninhibited.

'I'll have to take that robe off to do your shoulders,' he warned her, frowning a little as though he still couldn't quite believe his ears.

'I don't mind.' It wasn't quite true, little spirals of excitement were dancing through her, strangely elusive sensations that alternated between pleasure and fear. 'After all, you're not my stepfather, are you?' she added bravely, quivering under the look he shot her from suddenly darkened eyes.

'No, I'm not,' he agreed shortly. 'Stay there and I'll go and get the stuff.

'Solarcaine,' he told her several minutes later when he came back. 'I always keep some down here. My sister's kids tend to forget about sunburn until it's time to go to bed.'

'You've got a sister?'

'What did you expect? That I sprang fully formed from the Gorgon's head?' he taunted cynically. 'Yes, I have a sister; she's quite a lot older than me and is happily married to a G.P. They have four children ranging from twelve to twenty.'

It was the first time he had mentioned his family

to her, and Laurel felt a quiver of anguish that so much of his life was a closed book to her. And yet why should she feel that way?

'Sit up, Laurel, and I'll just slide the robe from your shoulders.'

She did as he instructed, amazed to discover how lightheaded she felt. Her head flopped heavily against his shoulder. He seemed to tense for a moment before easing the towelling away from her skin—skin which she admitted was beginning to sting painfully.

She closed her eyes as he started to smooth the cream into her shoulders. His touch soothed the pain, replacing it with ... with what? she wondered nervously as tiny tendrils of pleasure curled through her. Her hand which had been pressed flat against his robe seemed to find its way inside it to the warmth of his chest, her fingers curling hesitantly against its smoothness.

'Laurel?'

She barely caught the constraint in his voice, her soft 'mmm' making him demand roughly, 'You aren't going to sleep on me, are you?'

She opened her eyes drowsily, focusing on the tanned column of his throat. Her hand lay against his collarbone and she touched it tentatively, exploring the shape and feel of it.

'Does it matter if I do?' she asked him, yawning a little, still under the influence of the brandy he had given her.

'Only if you don't mind waking up in my arms—in my bed,' he told her bluntly. 'Is that what you want?'

Was it? Of course it wasn't! And yet as he re-capped the lotion he had been spreading into her shoulders and started to move away she clung to him, burying her face against his shoulder.

'Laurel!'

He said her name warily, grasping her chin and forcing it up so that she had to look at him. Her robe had come loose and revealed the upper curves of her breasts, but Laurel wasn't aware of it. What she was aware of was that for a moment in Oliver's arms she had experienced a comfort and sense of wellbeing dimly remembered from her childhood, and she didn't want to lose it.

'Don't leave me, Oliver,' she murmured softly. 'I want you to stay with me.'

'Do you?' His face was completely blank. 'I don't think you know what you're saying; what you're asking for—or do you, Laurel? Do you know very well what you're inviting? Very well. . . .'

His voice and expression had changed, alarm started to flutter inside her. She pulled away, but he was holding her arms and all her impotent little struggle did was to cause her robe to slide even further down her body.

She heard Oliver's indrawn breath, followed the direction of his gaze and saw that it was fastened on the exposed curves of her breasts, and fear drowned out any desire she had felt to remain with him.

'Oliver. . . .'

'No, Laurel,' he told her thickly. 'No, please. . . . Not this time.' His voice came thickly, his eyes hot as they roamed her body.

And numbly, as he lowered her back on the bed, keeping her there with his hands, Laurel fought to ignore the tremulous response shivering through her.

'I shall hate you. . . .' she began, but he merely shook his head.

'I promise you you won't,' he told her huskily. 'You won't, Laurel.'

He bent his head and his lips moved slowly over hers while his fingers eased the stiff tension from her neck.

'Put your arms round me,' he told her softly, and like someone under the influence of a hypnotic power she did so. He had shrugged off his robe, and his skin felt like rough satin beneath her palms. She wanted to touch it. Tentatively she explored his shoulders, shuddering delicately as his tongue traced the outline of her mouth. His arms which had been either side of her on the bed curled round her and on a shock wave of realisation she felt the abrasive pressure of his body hair against her skin.

'Laurel, Laurel, you don't know what you do to me,' she heard him mutter as he covered her mouth with his, plunging her into a wild vortex of sensation, her fingers curled achingly into his skin as his mouth lifted from hers and then moved seductively along her jaw, her throat, the sensitive hollow beneath her ear, each touch sending fierce tremors of pleasure through her body. Was this being frigid? She couldn't understand what was happening to her; the emotion Oliver's touch was arousing. Her robe was gone completely and now his fingers trailed strokingly across her stomach, his eyes watching her, gauging her response.

'Nice, isn't it?' he asked her throatily.

Her muscles tensed, but she couldn't deny what he was doing to her, how he was making her feel. Something flickered in his eyes, an emotion she couldn't name. She moaned faintly, and then his mouth closed over hers, damming her protests, stealing away her breath, carrying her with him to a place where only sensation existed, draining her of everything but the need to respond to the sorcery of his touch.

When his mouth left hers to trail seductively along her throat, she pressed her burning lips against his shoulder, gasping in shock as his fingers cupped her breast, stroking the sensitive flesh, his thumb moving arousingly over the nipple until it throbbed and ached with needs Laurel could barely understand. Without warning she had been flung into a vast alien ocean of unknown sensations; sensations she had never in her wildest dreams imagined existed; sensations that made her body ache and yearn to be closer to Oliver's. And it seemed that he sensed her need, because he drew her against his body, letting her feel the aroused heat of his thighs, making her tremble with an awareness of his maleness. And then he was holding her away from him, his face and body rigid with a tension that seemed to coil through her too, his expression oddly taut and tense.

What was he looking for? she wondered hesitantly.

'You aren't frigid, Laurel,' he told her softly, 'and you damned well know it!'

It was like a shower of icy water, 'No!' she cried bitterly. 'I. . . .'

'You responded to me,' he told her grittily,

'I. . . .' Slowly the mists were clearing; she remembered how she had fled from him; how he had threatened to turn her into a woman; just as he was doing now. She struggled to get away from him, loathing herself for the way she had reacted to his touch, but his fingers tightened in her hair, holding her beneath him.

'Stop fighting yourself, Laurel,' he told her softly. His mouth drifted kisses over each eyelid in turn and then trailed down to her mouth, playing tormentingly with the sensitive skin there until she was on fire with a need for his kiss. Everything else was forgotten, a slow agonising ache spreading upwards from her stomach, a deep groan wrenched from her throat as Oliver's mouth finally closed over hers.

His kisses were a potent, heady drug, depriving her of everything but the ability to respond to the emotion he aroused within her. There was no thought of stopping him in her mind when his hands slid slowly down her body to cup her breasts, and then he lowered his head, placing delicate butterfly kisses in the valley between her breasts.

He paused to look up at her and Laurel felt a tension in him that communicated itself to her. As though some unspoken message had passed between them, he groaned huskily and lowered his head, touching the aching tip of one breast with his tongue briefly before possessing it hungrily with his mouth in a caress that shattered all her preconceived conceptions of lovemaking.

Piercing sweet pleasure stormed through her, her fingers curled into his hair, holding him against her body; a body which arched in wilful complicity beneath him mutely pleading for the possession of his.

Floundering on a tidal flood of emotion, Laurel didn't grasp what was happening when Oliver suddenly stiffened, tensing his body as he lifted his head.

'I can hear a car,' he told her briefly. 'Who knows who it is.' He looked down into her wildly flushed face and languorous eyes and said lightly, 'Perhaps it's just as well that we were interrupted when we were . . . for both our sakes!' He slid off the bed and retrieved his robe, pulling it on casually while Laurel blushed harder and averted her eyes from the sleek masculinity of his body—a body which had been pressed intimately to every contour of hers!

After he had gone she simply lay there for several seconds, listening to the sound of the car drawing nearer, and then she started to tremble with reaction, hands pressed against her burning hot face. What on earth had she done? She felt hot and cold shudders tear at her, shame a sickness lodged in her stomach. What on earth had possessed her? What would Oliver think of her? Did he in fact think of her as a person at all, or was she simply an experiment? A cold dreadful recognition seeped through her veins. Was this how he intended to turn her into a woman—by making love to her? Could any man be so cold-blooded?

She heard the car pull up outside and disgorge several chattering passengers.

'Laurel, it's my sister and her family! 'You needn't bother coming down if you don't feel up to it, they're only making an overnight stop,' Oliver called up to her. Which roughly translated meant that it was a strictly family gathering and he would prefer her to absent herself from it, Laurel decided miserably, thumping her pillow and trying to forget how her wanton body had clung to and welcomed his.

She had come here for revenge, and yet instead. . . . Instead what? If she had responded to Oliver, couldn't that response have been fuelled by anger as much as desire? Anger such as she felt towards him was a powerful emotion, capable of playing odd tricks. Relief flooded through her. Of course, that was it: anger against him had triggered off her response to him. That was the explanation. That had to be the explanation.

CHAPTER SEVEN

LAUREL was awake and dressed early in the morning. Not because she was at all curious about Oliver's family, she assured herself as she set about making coffee and warming croissants in the oven.

The back door opened and she gave a start at finding herself confronted by two young men who were quite obviously as surprised to see her as she was them.

'Hi,' the younger of the two said with a grin. 'So you're Uncle Oliver's secretary. Wish I was a writer!'

So this was one of Oliver's nephews. The twenty-year-old, without doubt. His companion, who looked a couple of years older, smiled slowly at Laurel in a way which would have had her scuttling into her shell four short weeks ago, but now merely made her flush slightly.

'Stop it, Chas, you're embarrassing the poor girl. Don't mind my friend here—you'd think he'd never seen a pretty girl before. Look, we'd better introduce ourselves. I'm Richard, Oliver's nephew and this is a friend of mine, Charles Hawley. We've taken on a summer job—helping Ma look after the kids and a free holiday thrown in for us as a bonus. We're on our way down to Spain and decided to stop off here for the night. Ma gets all broody when her precious brother's been out of sight for too long. She worries that some fortune-hunting harpy is going to get her claws into him. A sucker for a hard-luck story, is Uncle O.'

Was he? That wasn't the impression Laurel had of him.

'Can we help at all?'

When Laurel shook her head, he grinned engagingly. 'In that case, Chas, I think we might just about have time for a swim before breakfast!'

Four children, Oliver had said his sister had, so that made eight of them altogether, Laurel decided, counting mentally as she got the table ready, unless of course as Oliver's secretary his sister might object if she ate with them. She gnawed her lip, frowning as she tried to decide what to do, and then shrugged. She would just have to play it by ear. She could always eat her breakfast later if it looked as though she wasn't welcome.

Half an hour later, Oliver on one side of her and his sister on the other, she admitted that she couldn't have been more wrong. Physically incredibly like her brother, Elizabeth Turner was a placid, cheerful woman in her mid-forties, who Laurel suspected it would take a great deal to stir to anger.

'So Graham can't make it this trip,' Oliver was saying to her. 'That's a pity.'

'Umm,' Elizabeth agreed, 'He could really do with the rest, but at least I've got the boys to help me.'

'You really think they will once they've seen what the beaches of Marbella have to offer?' Oliver drawled, cocking an eyebrow in the direction of his elder nephew.

Richard flushed, but Chas Hawley merely smiled at Laurel and went on with his breakfast. Although only a couple of years separated them, Chas was a far more sophisticated specimen. She had the impression that Oliver didn't like him, and

every time he addressed a comment to her, Oliver
intervened. Perhaps he didn't like the thought of
the paid help mingling with a guest of his family,
she thought bitterly, as she listened to Richard
explaining how he and Chas had become friendly
at university.

She liked these younger members of the Savage
family, she decided, watching them. Richard was
the eldest, but still very boyish, obviously hero-
worshipping his uncle, but intent on a medical
career like his father.

After him came the fifteen-year-old twins; boys
again, and as alike as two peas in a pod,
although unlike the others they were startlingly
fair.

'Paul and Robert take after their father,'
Elizabeth told Laurel, as she helped her clear away
the breakfast things. 'Richard and Anna are true
Savages, though. How do you like working for my
brother, by the way?' she asked. 'It can't be easy—
not knowing that temper of his.'

'It's very stimulating,' Laurel replied not
untruthfully. 'I enjoy it.'

'Umm—well, rather you than me. As I know to
my cost, he can be like a dog worrying a bone
when he gets his teeth into something, and never
more so when than he's working on a new book.
What's this one about?'

'I'm not quite sure—no, really,' Laurel protested
when Elizabeth's eyebrows rose. 'So far he's only
done the opening chapters, and they are exclusively
concerned with the main character—a man who's
suffering the burden of guilt for something that
happened in the past.'

'Well, knowing my brother, it will be another
runaway best-seller, but he deserves it, he puts
something of himself into each one of them. How

did you get the job?' Elizabeth asked curiously. 'He doesn't normally employ a secretary.'

'I asked if I could work for him,' Laurel admitted.

'And I said she could,' Oliver finished for her, walking into the kitchen and surprising them both. 'Beth, I'm afraid your offspring are beginning to get bored,' he told his sister. 'It's unfortunate that on the one day you choose to visit me the mistral starts to blow, but if you like we could take a trip into Arles this afternoon.'

'As long as I keep them out of your way this morning?' his sister suggested dryly. 'Very well, although I do think it's too bad of you to work today, Oliver. We don't see that much of you.'

'Unfortunate, but necessary,' he told her briefly. 'Inspiration and all that, my dear sister!'

He was gone before she could retort. 'Men!' she groaned heavily to Laurel, 'and Oliver is quite the most exasperating example of the breed! Still, I suppose we'd better do as he says. I think I'll set the kids to tidying up the living room a little bit, that should keep them quiet until lunchtime.'

A little to her surprise Laurel discovered that Oliver had taken his work upstairs with him.

'Oh, he knows what to expect by now when we're around,' Elizabeth told her with a grin. 'He's never forgiven me for letting the twins eat one of his precious manuscripts when they were babies, so now whenever we descend on him he moves everything out of the way. Good heavens, just look at the dust on these shelves, Laurel! I suppose he banned you from touching them, did he?'

Laurel nodded. Oliver had made it very clear from the start that as far as he was concerned the living room was strictly out of bounds as far as any tidying up went.

'Well, we'll start with these. Goodness, will you just look at this!' she exclaimed as she opened the door of one of the lower cupboards and a mass of typed papers fell out.

'I think I'd better let you sort through that lot,' she said, passing them over to Laurel. 'I'll let the twins do the bookshelves, that should keep them quiet for an hour or so—who knows,' she added humorously, 'they might even take it into their heads to open the odd one. At the moment they're sports mad; I'm hoping they'll grow out of it.'

Laurel smiled absently. The bundle of papers Elizabeth had passed to her were dated six years previously. She picked up the first one. It was an article about the Middle East; beneath it was one about the fors and againsts of private education; there were others, but Laurel barely glanced at them, her hands shaking when she eventually came to what she was seeking.

Yes, this was the one . . . the typescript blurred as she read her own name. She must have made an odd choking sound before Elizabeth was at her side suddenly, concern in her voice as she asked if she was all right. And then she too looked down at the papers.

'Oh, Laurel,' she said softly. 'My dear, I had no idea . . . you are that girl, aren't you? I thought your name was familiar. Oh my poor child! So Oliver found you after all. . . . I can remember it all so vividly. Our parents were still alive then, although our cousin's death had struck them a bad blow. He was like a third child to them, you see. He was always terrified of his own parents, poor boy. They wanted so much for him. . . .' she sighed. 'That was the tragedy of it, really, if they hadn't set him such impossibly high standards. . . .

'Oliver blamed himself for what happened to

him. That girl—the one he was involved with—
Oliver will have told you about it—she had been a
girl-friend of Oliver's at one time, but unlike poor
Peter he had no delusions as to what she was. I
believe she actually intimated to Peter that Oliver
had seduced her! And of course he believed her,
initially at least.

'When Peter died Oliver changed; we all noticed
it, and my mother especially worried about it.
Journalists possess such power, she used to say to
him, and unless they could use it wisely and
without bias they shouldn't use it at all. I think she
worried that something might happen—and then
of course it did.

'Did Oliver tell you that she begged him to see
you himself and talk to you? She was convinced
that you weren't lying, but Oliver wouldn't listen.
He always was stubborn and headstrong. He was
so convinced that he was right, and not even
Mother could sway him.

'Of course later, when he did discover the truth,
the enormity of what he'd done almost broke him.
He swore then that he was giving up journalism.
He swore that he'd make it up to you somehow;
searched everywhere for you; tried to persuade his
paper to print a different story, but they refused—
told him that to do so would damage his
credibility and with it theirs. Journalists aren't
allowed to admit to mistakes, was what they said
to him. He's always been a very compassionate
person, even as a small child. I think he found it
almost impossible to live with what he'd done. It
seemed to eat into him ... but now he's found
you, and. . . .' She looked at Laurel thoughtfully.
'How do you feel about him? Do you resent him?'

How could she tell Elizabeth the truth? And yet
somehow she couldn't lie to her either. She bit her

lip, worrying at the soft flesh her eyes dark with pain.

'I accept that he did what he did in good faith,' she managed at last. 'My stepfather was an accomplished liar, even my mother, who had witnessed what happened, preferred to believe him rather than me.'

The arrival of the twins put an end to their conversation, and while their mother instructed them as to what they were to do, Laurel picked up the articles and carried them up to her room. A compassionate man, and one whose credibility could be destroyed if the truth were ever exposed. Wasn't that the weapon she was looking for? She trembled, leaning against the armoire. What was the matter with her? Was she such a coward that now that the knife was in her hand she couldn't use it?

It had been decided that they would set out for Arles immediately after an early lunch. Oliver had some shopping he wanted to do—some books he needed, he told Laurel, and to her amazement he told her that he wanted her to go with them.

'But it's a family party,' she began awkwardly, flushing vividly as he looked at her and she remembered the intimacy that party had interrupted. His look seemed to remind her of it too.

'You're coming with us,' he told her firmly, and when she said lightly, 'Another step on the way to womanhood—like last night?' he looked at her levelly and agreed expressionlessly, 'If that's how you want to see it—yes.'

For some reason she seemed to have annoyed him. He had seemed angry at lunchtime when she chatted to Richard; Laurel frowned over the thought.

'Chas and I have our own car,' Richard told her. 'Why don't you ride with us?'

She hadn't realised that Oliver was standing behind them until she heard him say freezingly. 'Richard, Laurel is my secretary and here to work, not play.' His swift change of mood startled her, although she managed to conceal it.

When Richard had disappeared he said to her softly, 'I thought it was steps you were taking, Laurel, timidly and nervously, not leaps—and certainly not with my nephew,' he told her with a harsh brutality that stung.

What was he trying to say? That she was flirting with Richard? Why, it was ridiculous! They had been talking. . . .

He saw her heading for the stairs and called after her, 'While you're up there will you bring my jacket down for me, it's on the bed.'

She entered his room hesitantly. Evidence of his morning's work lay all round him. He had been using a portable typewriter, and she frowned. She hadn't realised he could do his own typing. The sheets lay face down on the bed and she picked them up, straightening them. As she did so the first few works caught her eye.

'Physical responses,' she read, her eyes widening as she took in the import of what she was reading. 'Excellent when caught off guard; or emotions unlocked, i.e. anger; fear still there, but whether of self or past unknown.'

There were other notes, notes that made it sickeningly clear that Oliver was, as she had first suspected, writing about her; using her. Her eyes moved swiftly over the typewritten page, but she couldn't take in any more. She was in no doubt that Oliver intended to use her in his novel. That was why he had brought her here, and she had been right all along. His claim that he intended to restore her to womanhood was simply a cloak for his real intentions, which were to delve into her personality to suck it dry for his book, revealing every vulnerable corner of her mind and heart.

'Laurel!'

His voice from downstairs reminded her that it would be foolish to let him see that she had guessed the truth. Snatching up his coat, she hurried downstairs, her mind seething feverishly with thoughts.

What was she going to do? Her initial thought was that she should leave, today—but if she did that she wouldn't be able to be revenged on him as she had planned. But there must be something she could do. Refuse to participate in any more of his experiments? Oh, what a fool she had been last night . . . actually deceiving herself that there was comfort to be found in his arms; that they represented some form of sanctuary, when all the time. . . . She bit down hard on her lip, almost drawing blood as she tried to banish her boiling hatred from her eyes before she walked into the living room. He mustn't guess what she had seen.

'You were up there a long time.'

Her senses, now almost supernaturally attuned to his, searched the words for some hidden meaning.

'I was brushing my hair,' she lied, turning her back on him. 'Here's your coat.'

She felt sure he was watching her more keenly than usual, but then perhaps she had never noticed before how closely he studied her. After all, that was all she was to him—a specimen; something to be analysed for his precious book. Well, she would show him! If she had hated him before it was nothing compared to what she felt now!

The mistral blew grittily all the way to Arles. Laurel couldn't remember when she had last felt so irritable, but then she had good reason, hadn't she?

Arles itself was beautiful, shimmering in the sun, rosy glowing pantiled roofs, a painter's dream. Fortunately it was still too early in the season for it to be busy, and as Oliver parked the Ferrari behind his sister's Range Rover, Laurel prepared to make her escape. She wasn't going to have him watching her all afternoon, storing up her reactions, tabulating them as he had done when he made love to her. Made love.... Colour brushed her skin. He hadn't been making love to her, she acknowledged bitterly. He had been using her, just as he had used her once before.

She shot out of the car the moment it stopped, determined to make it clear that she intended to spend the afternoon alone.

'Just where do you think you're going?'

Oliver's voice stopped her before she had taken more than half a dozen steps.

'You seem to forget you're in my employ,' he told her tersely. 'If you'd any ideas about spending the afternoon with my nephew and his friend, then forget them. We need to re-stock with food. You can do that for a start, and I don't suppose my sister would object to someone keeping an eye on Anna for her.'

'So now I'm a housekeeper and nanny as well as a secretary, am I?' Laurel stormed at him. 'You seem to forget that I haven't had any time off since I started to work for you, and if I want to spend this afternoon....' 'Alone,' she had been about to say, but she paused and substituted instead ... 'doing my own thing, you aren't going to stop me!'

'Like hell,' Oliver told her brutally. She backed away from him unsteadily, realising that somehow she had unleashed that temper Elizabeth had been telling her about. She had never seen him angry, really angry, before, but she whipped up her own temper, reminding herself of what she had read, warning herself that she must not allow herself to be bullied by this man.

'Oliver, what on earth's going on?' Neither of them had seen Elizabeth approach and she looked at them curiously. 'You two aren't quarrelling, are you?'

'To quarrel requires a degree of intimacy Laurel and I don't possess,' he told his sister dryly. 'No, we weren't quarrelling. I've got some errands to do, so I suggest that we all go our separate ways and then meet up again here in the square in a couple of hours.'

'Oh, I thought we could all explore the Roman amphitheatre together!' Elizabeth exclaimed, looking disappointed.

Laurel felt dreadful when Oliver announced sardonically. 'Yes–well, Laurel prefers to make her own explorations, doubtless of a different nature from ours, and as I said, I have some errands of my own, so. . . .'

Somehow Laurel discovered that when they did eventually go their own separate ways, Chas Hawley had attached himself to her.

'I thought you would have wanted to stay with Richard,' she pointed out to him as he suggested that they team up for the afternoon.

'Oh, Rick's okay in his way.' He shrugged his shoulders. 'A little immature, though; and rather too juvenile in his hero-worship of Uncle O. for my taste sometimes. You must get as bored with it as I do. Look, why don't we make an evening of it? Eat out somewhere, go to a club . . . a last taste of freedom for me before I start baby-sitting.'

Laurel wasn't too sure that she cared for the

way he put down Richard, or his family. From what she had gathered Chas had had no plans for his holiday until Richard had suggested he accompany them, and she also suspected that Elizabeth was hardly likely to be the kind of mother who would genuinely expect two young men to look after her younger children. No, she had had the distinct impression that the holiday job was merely an excuse to give both young men a cheap vacation, and she disliked Chas's way of intimating that he was doing the Turners a favour when she suspected the boot was on the other foot. Still, his company was probably better than being on her own, and she suspected it had annoyed Oliver to see them walk away together. Perhaps that would teach him that she was perfectly capable of making a few experiments of her own, she thought hardily.

'Well, how about it?' Chas encouraged. 'We're not leaving until the morning, we could make quite a night of it.'

'I'm not sure,' she hesitated. 'Let's leave it until later shall we. You never know,' she smiled mischievously, 'you might have had enough of me by the end of the afternoon!'

'I doubt it.'

She wasn't sure if she liked the way he was looking at her. It reminded her too much of another look—her stepfather's look, she acknowledged with a shiver. Were all men like that? Greedy and selfish?

As though he sensed her withdrawal, Chas didn't refer to the subject again during the afternoon. He had an irreverent sense of humour which sometimes she found jarring but more often than not made her laugh, and it was only as they returned to the square that she realised she had

spent the entire afternoon with a young male she
would have run a mile from only a short time ago.
Compared with Oliver he presented no threat at
all. Compared with Oliver. She stumbled, and
trembled a little. Why was she comparing him with
Oliver? Oliver Savage meant nothing to her.
Nothing! But he had made it possible for her to
enjoy the company of a young man for an
afternoon without shaking with terror. If he was
using her then he had given her something too . . .
she couldn't deny that!

They were the last to return to the square. Chas
had slipped an arm round her shoulders when she
stumbled, and more to prove to herself how much
better she was than any other reason, she had
allowed it to remain there, so that the first view of
the others had of them was the pair of them linked
together by Chas's arm, as they rounded the
corner.

'You're late,' Oliver announced tersely. 'We've
been waiting for you.'

'Only five minutes Oliver,' Elizabeth interrupted
mildly. 'Don't get in such a flap! I told you there
was nothing to worry about. . . .'

'That's right. Laurel's perfectly safe with me,'
Chas agreed, giving Laurel a proprietorial hug. 'So
safe that she's going to let me wine and dine her
tonight, aren't you?'

She was just about to refuse, when her eye was
caught by the pile of books on the table.
Psychology books. Books that Oliver intended to
use to delve even deeper into her mind? she
wondered bitterly. Well, he had wasted his money.
She wasn't going to let him.

'Is this true?' he demanded, rounding on her,
his mouth thinning. 'Are you planning to spend
the evening with him?'

'Yes,' she told him blithely, astonished at the sheer sense of exultation the word gave her. She knew he didn't want her to go, but it gave her infinite pleasure to defy him, especially when she knew why he didn't want her to go. She was a specimen, an 'experiment', and nothing was to be allowed to become between him and the final results—results he obviously needed for his new book.

'I hope you know what you're doing,' was all he finally said, adding later in a voice that only she could hear, 'Be careful, Laurel. Wanting to leave the past behind you is fine; trying to catch up on six years' living all in one go is another. You're still very much at the toddler stage, you know . . . when it comes to sex, that is. You know what all the moves are, but you still haven't learned to co-ordinate them—I should hate to see you fall flat on your face.' His false assumption of concern for her doubled her fury.

'If I do, Chas will be there to catch me, won't he?' she retorted sweetly, astonished to see the white ring of anger round his mouth.

'Perhaps your stepfather wasn't lying after all,' was his final brutal thrust. 'Perhaps you are asking for it!'

It was six o'clock before the others left to return to the farmhouse. Oliver's sister wanted an early start in the morning and Chas promised that they wouldn't be late. 'Arles isn't exactly Paris, is it?' he asked ruefully. 'I expect the whole place shuts down at ten.'

Alone with him, Laurel wasn't quite so sure that defying Oliver had been a good idea. For one thing, his manner towards her changed quite markedly. His arm resting on her shoulders was far more intimate than she would have liked, and she moved away from him when it slipped to her arm, his fingers brushing the curve of her breast.

His eyebrows rose. 'I wouldn't have thought you were such a prude,' he commented. 'Not after living with a man like Savage.'

'Living with? I'm Oliver's secretary, that's all,' Laurel told him indignantly. 'I think you've got the wrong idea, Chas.'

'Oh, I don't think so,' he argued lazily. 'In fact I'm sure not. You can say what you like, Laurel, but there was something distinctly possessive about the way he told you he didn't want you coming out with me tonight. And no man gets like that with a woman unless she gives him good cause.'

'Oliver, was just ... concerned about me,' she told him stiffly.

'Sure he was,' he agreed, laughing coarsely, 'concerned that someone else might be fishing what he considers private waters. It's time he learned that modern girls don't belong exclusively to one man, isn't that right? And I'm all for it.'

She could imagine! Angry with him, Laurel pulled away. 'You're quite wrong, Chas,' she told him. 'I'm just Oliver's secretary, nothing more.'

'Is that so? Then how come when we arrived last night there was only one light on? One bedroom light, that is. It wasn't until we were almost up to the house that any downstairs lights went on. You know what that suggests to me, Laurel?'

She did, and she knew it would be a waste of time trying to explain to him what had actually happened. Not that it was really any of his business.

'No, and I don't want to,' she told him tightly. 'Chas, I think tonight was a bad idea. I'd like to go back to the farmhouse now.'

'And let Uncle O. know that you prefer him to me? No way, baby,' he told her cruelly. 'I'm sick of hearing Rick ramble on about his precious uncle. Seems to me the guy's bigheaded enough already without you adding to it. I could give you a good time. . . .'

Laurel felt sick. Oliver had been right to warn her against him.

'No, thanks,' she said shakily. 'I'd really much rather go back, Chas.'

His eyes narrowed, and she became aware of the petulant droop to his mouth and the glittering excitement in his eyes as they moved restlessly over her.

'What's the matter?' he taunted. 'Afraid I might not be as generous as Savage?'

It was obvious that he wasn't going to take her back, and his mood frightened her. Perhaps if they had something to eat and then left. . . . Yes, that was the best thing.

Only she didn't bargain for the carafe of wine which was brought to their table, or that Chas would insist on drinking all of it himself when she refused more after discovering that it was a little sour and rough for her taste.

When they left the restaurant it was almost ten o'clock. Chas wanted to look for a club or a bar, but Laurel insisted that she wanted to return to the farmhouse.

'Okay,' he agreed, leering at her. 'Gives me longer to stop for a while on the way back, doesn't it?'

They were halfway back to the farmhouse when he pulled off down a narrow country road. It was completely dark, the countryside deserted, and Laurel felt a quiver of fear as he switched off the engine and turned towards her.

'Relax,' he told her, feeling her tense as he slid his arm round her. 'What's the panic?'

'Elizabeth will be wondering where we are,' she objected. 'You know she's planning an early start in the morning!'

'Elizabeth will object? Don't you mean Savage will object?' he demanded. 'Look, what is it with you, going out with one guy but with your mind constantly on another? I thought we could have fun together.'

'You invited me out for a meal,' Laurel reminded him bitterly.

'Yeah, but we both know what that implies.'

'That I have to pay for it?' Laurel challenged bitterly. 'Well, I'm sorry, Chas, but you picked the wrong girl.'

She pulled away from him, pushing open the car door, stumbling down the rutted track as she headed for the main road. Behind her she heard him curse and then start the engine. He drew alongside her.

'Aw, come on, Laurel, don't be such a prude!' he wheedled, his tone changing and hardening when she refused to respond. 'What is it with you anyway?' he demanded roughly. 'You know what it's all about.'

His rough tone and hard eyes unnerved her. She wished she had never accepted his invitation; never seen those books of Oliver's. If she hadn't she'd be safe at the farmhouse by now.

Safe! A curious sensation fluttered through her stomach, a persistent shiver of alarm feathering along her nerves, but before she could correctly interpret the warning they were trying to give her, Chas suddenly slammed the car angrily into second gear and screamed past her, covering her in fine dust.

'You want Savage,' he threw at her above the protesting whine of the engine. 'Okay, then let him take you home!'

He couldn't really mean to leave her here, Laurel thought, appalled, several seconds later, searching the road for some evidence that he meant to turn back. But his tail-lights had already disappeared— in the direction of Arles, not the farmhouse—and she was alone, who knew how many miles from the nearest habitation. Terrified sobs rose in her throat, but she suppressed them. There was nothing to be gained from giving way to her emotions. Thankful that she had chosen to wear her flat-heeled sandals, she started to plod wearily in the direction of the farmhouse. Surely somewhere along the way there must be somewhere she could get help?

The night was full of sounds, frightening at first, but comforting after a while when she had learned to distinguish them. The mistral had gone, leaving the air soft and scented with mimosa.

Suddenly behind her she heard the sound of a car approaching. Oliver—please let it be Oliver, was the irrational thought that first burst upon her. She turned, disappointment flooding over her when she realised the car wasn't Oliver's Ferrari, and neither was it heading in her direction; it had turned off before it reached her, but Laurel was more concerned with the gaping chasm which suddenly appeared to have opened under her feet than the disappearance of the car.

It was only natural that she should feel relief, joy even, at the thought of being spared the ordeal of her long walk, but the emotions which had swept over her when she first thought the car might be Oliver's hadn't been those simple basic feelings.

In those brief telling seconds she had run the gamut of a whole range of feelings—incredible joy; tremulous uncertainty, hope, pleasure, and most of all. . . .

Most of all what?

She sat down suddenly, shivering and trembling with reaction as she battled against the truth and tried to analyse her emotions. She had wanted that car to be Oliver's; had yearned desperately to see him striding towards her, taking her in his arms, holding her safe.

A conflicting surge of emotion engulfed her. She felt as though she had lost touch with everything familiar; as though her entire world had suddenly been turned upside down. She had come to Provence with Oliver with the sole purpose of wounding him; of inflicting on him the pain she had herself endured, and instead. . . .

Instead she was in danger of suffering a far greater pain herself; the anguish of loving a man and knowing her love would never be returned.

She loved Oliver! Admitting it brought a certain peace; so many irrationalities in her own behaviour were explained once she had admitted it. No wonder she had been so reluctant to read those articles; to get on with her self-imposed task.

But she must! She mustn't let what she felt for him distract her from her purpose. The fact of her loving him changed nothing. She had come to Provence for a reason and she must see it through. She must!

But how could she? All along she had felt a warring distaste for what she planned to do. Her conscience had consistently troubled her; and now she had to fight against her love as well. While her pride urged retaliation her heart whispered a different message, even hinting that all along, secretly her desire to be with Oliver had sprung not from any desire for revenge, but a simple need to be with the man she loved.

She had been so bitter, so engrossed in the past that she hadn't been able to recognise her own emotions, and every minute spent with Oliver had only made matters worse, she now recognised. His compassion, his concern, his probing questions, all these had helped breach her defences, making her more vulnerable, although she had tried to hide that fact from herself by cloaking her vulnerability with anger.

Walking had become an automatic reaction not requiring any thought; all her mental concentration focusing on the discovery of her love.

When had it first started? When he walked into the office, or earlier? Did it perhaps have its roots in the very first encounter; had the seeds of trust and warmth sown then not after all been destroyed in the conflagration of his betrayal? Had they survived and lain dormant all through the years waiting for his reappearance into her life to put out shoots?

Had she buried her true feelings, encasing them in the frigidity she had used to stop herself from being hurt again?

And then when they had met all that emotion had come rushing to the surface, breaking through the ice.

But she must not give way to it. Good heavens, if he were to guess how she felt! He would have a field day, she told herself bitterly, thinking of the textbooks she had seen. Could he have guessed? She started to tremble convulsively.

She had to get away from him. She had to. She couldn't trust herself any longer. A sob tore at her throat. It was all so unfair. Oliver was going to use her again while she, hampered by her love, couldn't even bring herself to use the puny weapons she had at her disposal to fight back. If she had any pride, she would carry out her original plan, she lashed herself bitterly. She owed it to herself to wipe out the past and start again. How could she possibly start again now? She stopped again, acknowledging with a faint sense of disbelieving shock that somewhere deep down inside her lurked the primeval notion that somehow by punishing Oliver, by hurting him, she would 'buy' her own freedom from the past and all the nightmares it still held. She had never thought of herself as particularly superstitious, but her reasoning here was as primitive as those of the tribes who still believed that by using a 'sin-eater' and paying him they could shed their own failings and guilt. She had thought that by hurting Oliver she could wipe out her own hurt, but she saw now that burdened by her love for him, she would only be hurt the more.

Damn, she had to get away! If she didn't she might easily betray herself, weakened as she was by her need of him.

Slowly, mechanically she walked on, glancing at her watch occasionally, trying to still the thoughts that tormented her. There was no sign of human habitation. The road from the farm-house to Arles was a quiet country one, she remembered, and she realised with dismay that she hadn't seen any other building on the way. How much farther was it to the farmhouse? Had Chas returned, and how had he explained away her absence? Why hadn't anyone come to look for her? Why didn't she have the pride to do as she had first intended? Why was she so weak? The thoughts beat at her unceasingly until she sank exhausted by the roadside, clenched fists pressed bitterly to her throbbing forehead as her thoughts chased one another unceasingly through her aching head.

CHAPTER EIGHT

SHE woke up with a start, horrified to discover that she had fallen asleep by the side of the road. Her body felt gritty from the dust; her hair untidy, and her clothes grubby. A false dawn was just beginning to tinge the sky, and she shivered a little with the cool air.

Why had no one come to look for her? Surely Chas must have returned from Arles by now? Somehow she managed to force her tired legs to move. It was too cold to simply sit around and wait for help to arrive, and before she had gone more than half a mile Laurel realised that she was closer to the farmhouse than she had realised, maybe only five miles or so away.

Walking gave her time to consider and analyse her feelings towards Oliver. She knew she loved him, but why? Because she had trusted him once, briefly, as an adolescent? No. That must have some part of it, she suspected. Had he not already been known to her; had her six-year-old resentment towards him not sparked off an anger which overcame all her normal reticence, she would never have allowed her emotions to get so out of control that she could feel anything for him. That had been the starting point, and there had been something in the way he had listened, understood—or so she had thought all those years ago—which had lingered, providing the basis for what she now felt for him. But it was more than that. Unbelievably, with Oliver she felt no sexual fear—oh, there were times when his features blurred and her mind turned inwards and saw only her stepfather, but Oliver himself induced neither sexual dread or even the revulsion she had come to expect whenever a member of the male sex approached her. Quite the opposite. Her stomach muscles quivered softly as she remembered how she had felt. She had wanted him to touch her; had wanted to touch him. Rachel had told her that one day it would happen, but she had never believed it.

But Oliver wasn't a god, he was a living, breathing human being, a compassionate and caring one, if she was to believe his sister, and strangely she did believe her. Even at that first meeting she had sensed the lack of cruelty in him, although later events had destroyed her trust in her own adolescent judgment. But he didn't love her. And he was using her. So if she had any sense she would take herself as far away from him as she possibly could, and the sooner the better.

Strange how her normal defence system didn't seem to be functioning properly. Instead of wanting to leave she had a weak-willed desire to stay. She even began to wonder feverishly, as she walked, what it would be like to know the full pleasure of his possession—and pleasure it would be. She shivered a little, remembering the brush of his skin against hers, dazed by the knowledge that if such a brief contact could induce such a delirium of longing, to be held in his arms with no barriers between them must be the very zenith of delight.

Lost in her thoughts as she was, it was some time before she realised the low humming sound intruding on them was a car, and that it was coming up behind her very fast. She paused and half turned, unable to prevent a tremulous smile of relief when she realised it was Oliver's Ferrari and that he was driving it.

He drew up several yards ahead of her in a screech of tyres and a cloud of dust, which choked her of breath as she hurried towards him.

'Where the hell have you been?' he demanded furiously. 'I suppose it amuses you to realise that I've just spent half the night scouring Arles for you—enquiring at every seedy, run-down bar I could find because I was worried that young Chas might have taken you there against your will! To look at you now I can only assume that you were very willing indeed! You do realise, I suppose, that as you're my employee, it might have been courteous to tell me that you intended to spend the night with your lover, and not simply leave me to surmise that fact, when he rang us to say that he wasn't coming back and that he'd meet up with my sister in Marbella. I suppose I ought to be thankful that you came back at all—and after only one night, although by the looks of you it was an extremely busy one!'

'Chas rang you from Arles?' Laurel asked faintly. 'But. . . .'

'At two o'clock this morning,' Oliver agreed roughly, 'after the pair of you had had me half out of my mind with worry!'

'You were worried . . . about me?'

'Oh, for Pete's sake don't play games with me, Laurel! Of course I was worried about you! You may be way, way over the age of consent, but if you've consented with anyone other than Chas before, I'll be one very surprised man. But when you decide to do something, you don't do it by half measures, do you? And with him! But then I suppose your lack of experience goes some way to excusing your lack of taste.'

'Oliver, I haven't been with Chas. We had a quarrel. He left me. . . .'

'Oh yeah! Look, I'm not your father, Laurel, you don't have to lie to me. If you want to sleep with Chas that's your affair, but a little consideration wouldn't have come amiss!'

He looked angry, more angry than Laurel had ever seen him before, and no wonder, if he had driven to Arles and back looking for her. She was surprised that he had bothered. Unless, of course, he thought that any relationship she had with Chas might spoil his 'experiment', she reflected bitterly.

'Get in the car,' he told her grimly. He made no attempt to touch her, and Laurel didn't know if it was because he feared if he did he might strike her or because the thought of touching her now was abhorrent to him.

She had barely scrambled inelegantly in when he slammed the door behind her and stormed round to the driver's side. He got in without a word and switched on the engine. The car jolted forward, but had barely gone more than ten yards when he brought it to an abrupt halt. She half expected him to tell her to get out and walk, but instead he leaned towards her, and just for a moment he was Chas. She shrank back, hating the cynical, knowing look in his eyes as he said in a low voice,

'Oh no, Laurel, you're quite safe. I don't make love in cars, and even if I did. . . .' His eyes roamed her untidy appearance comprehensively, telling her that desire was the last thing he was likely to feel for her, especially sufficient to overrule his scruples about making love in cars.

'I merely wish to fasten this,' he told her, flicking up the metal tag of the seat-belt and pulling it across her. For a moment she felt the warmth of his hand against her breast. Her heart leapt into her throat and a fierce heat engulfed her.

Unlike Oliver, she recognised in shame, she would have been more than delighted to make love here and now. She found the knowledge both shocking and exciting.

'The mood I'm in right now isn't conducive to leisurely driving,' Oliver continued bitingly, 'so in order that I won't have the destruction of your body on my conscience as well as. . . .

'Irrational of me, isn't it?' he agreed with self-derision, 'but you see, Laurel, I had a rather special reason for hoping that your chrysalis would remain intact for just a little while longer. Obviously I was hoping for too much. Still, all is not lost. You have returned, and I have work to do . . . that is, if you have any energy left for work!'

And work they did! Oliver had prepared copious notes that he wanted her to type, and Laurel, who had barely done more than snatch a few brief hours' sleep, had a pounding headache by lunchtime. Oliver was still working on the opening chapters of his book; the main character was shaping well, and still elusively familiar. Did he intend to use her in this book, Laurel wondered, or another? Tension crackled in the atmosphere as they worked, Oliver pacing the room as he dictated, impatient and crackling with a fierce energy she had never seen before, as though a special kind of anger fuelled his thoughts.

'That's enough for today,' he told her at lunchtime. 'I suggest you spend this afternoon sleeping off last night.'

Because of the way he had said it, exhausted though she was Laurel refused to give in to her tiredness and go to bed. Instead she changed into her bikini, and was pleased to note that her body was beginning to tan. Although she still felt selfconscious in the tiny scraps of silk she was nowhere near as uncomfortable as she had been, and picking up her robe, she headed for the pool.

It wasn't until she reached the sheltered paved area that she realised that Oliver was already there, swimming powerfully towards her, so that it was impossible for her to leave without him being aware of it.

He looked up at her as he hauled himself out of the water.

'I didn't realise you were here.' Her voice sounded stilted and strained. It was a physical effort for her to drag her eyes away from his torso, tanned and water-sleek, drops of moisture clinging to the whorls of hair on his chest.

'Disappointed to find that I am? Don't worry, I shan't stop you daydreaming about Chas, if that's what you had in mind.' He leaned forward, reaching for a towel, tall and overpowering, exuding a maleness that turned her knees to jelly, and she longed to deny his accusations, but she knew that he would't believe her. Tears stung her eyes and she turned away, stumbling into one of the sun-loungers.

Oliver swore as he reached for her, swinging her off her feet as he grasped her upper arms, her eyes on a level with the pulse beating in the dark column of his throat. A terrible longing to reach out and touch him consumed her, as heat licked through her veins. She made a half-inarticulate murmur, which he obviously misintepreted.

'It's all right, Laurel,' he told her with a savagery that matched his name. 'I'm not going to touch you.'

I know, she wanted to cry, but I want you to . . . desperately!

When he had released her she lay down on the lounger, rolling on to her stomach and closing her eyes, trying to feign a relaxed pose but in reality tensely aware of every movement of the indolently male body next to her.

From beneath her lashes she watched Oliver smearing cream on his shoulders, and her tongue moved moistly over her dry lips as she followed the lines of his body, trembling with the intensity of her desire to touch him.

She had never in her wildest imagining believed it was possible to feel this depth of desire; this hunger that gnawed and burned; this need to know every inch of another's body, so strong and compulsive that it was physically painful subduing it.

'What about you?'

Her eyes flickered open. He was lying on a towel watching her. 'Your skin, Laurel, or don't you mind burning?'

'I've put some on already,' she managed to murmur.

'Then do my back for me, will you?' he asked her, tossing her the bottle and rolling over on to his side.

For a moment she contemplated refusing, but what if he should question why? Dry-mouthed, she uncapped the lotion and poured some into her palm, slowly spreading it on to his skin, her movements hesitant and uncertain, but as the shape and feel of his flesh became imprinted on her palms her shyness dissolved in the wonder of touching him. Her fingertips moved feather-light across his back, touching, learning.

Engrossed in her task, she wasn't aware of how still Oliver had gone until she reached the narrow curve of his waist, and then his tension communicated itself to her. Startled, she hesitated, her voice uncertain as she asked, 'Is something wrong?'

He swivelled round to stare at her with eyes almost black with derision, 'Oh, for Pete's sake Laurel, he rasped. 'Save those sort of games for Chas if you must, but don't use them on me—I don't like being teased. I'll say this,' he added brutally, 'either he's a damned good teacher or you're a quick learner. That was almost good enough to be professional!'

And before she could speak he stood up and dived cleanly into the water, doing a vigorous crawl for several lengths, while Laurel watched mutely from the poolside, wondering what she had done to make him so angry.

She was just preparing their evening meal when he walked into the kitchen and announced that he didn't want anything.

'I'm going into Arles,' he told her without adding any explanation. 'I don't know what time I'll be back. Don't wait up for me,' he added sardonically.

Alone, she went up to her room and tried to convince herself that love, without warmth and encouragement, was something that must surely die. Her eye was caught by her notebook, and she read through it, smiling wryly, as she read what she had written. How naïve she had been then! Actually thinking she was motivated only by revenge! The articles she had brought upstairs were there too, and she started to read through them, gaining a new insight into the man she loved as she did so. There was compassion, a deep compassion, and caring too, and tears blurred her eyes to think that there was so little of it to spare for her. They had got off on the wrong foot and

seemed destined to stay that way. Oliver always
seemed to be making misjudgments of her—odd in
such a shrewd man, almost as though where she
was concerned he wasn't completely unbiased in
his thinking.

She had just washed her hair and finished drying
it when she heard the Ferrari returning. It was
almost eleven o'clock. She heard Oliver unlocking
the car and walking to the door. Her bedroom
overlooked it, and she peeped out, frowning as she
saw him searching through his pockets, obviously
looking for his key.

As though he sensed her presence he glanced up,
and even though she moved back from the window
he had seen her.

'Come down and let me in, Laurel,' he
commanded. 'I can't find my key.'

She had stripped to her bra and briefs to wash
her hair, and snatched up the first thing that came
to hand—a candy-striped nightshirt which had
been amongst the things he had bought her,
quickly pulling it on and buttoning it as she
hurried downstairs.

The first thing Laurel noticed about him as she
opened the door was that he had been drinking.
She could smell it on his breath.

'You're quite safe,' he told her sardonically,
catching her expression. 'I'm not drunk. My
sorrows are doused rather than drowned.'

'I'm surprised you've got any,' Laurel retorted,
as he followed her into the kitchen.

'Why? Aren't I allowed human failings Laurel?'

His voice was bitter, and she didn't know him in
this strange mood.

'Would you like something to eat?' she asked
hesitantly. 'It wouldn't take long. . . .'

'Oh yes, it would,' he contradicted throatily. 'I

have a hunger that couldn't be quickly appeased, Laurel.' He laughed shortly. 'Oh, for Pete's sake stop looking at me like the wide-eyed innocent we both know you aren't any longer, and go back to bed, before I say something we'll both regret!'

Laurel was torn between staying and going. In the end, after one last uncertain glance at the hunched male figure, she fled. She didn't understand why Oliver had been drinking—perhaps it was something he needed to do to help relieve the tension that built up when he was writing. She did know that he wasn't drunk, but she feared the leashed brooding violence she sensd simmering below the surface, and had no wish to be the one to set a tinder to it, however inadvertently.

She was just getting into bed when she heard Oliver come upstairs and go into the bathroom. There was a sound of cupboards being opened and closed then he opened the door and called out, 'Laurel, have you any aspirin?'

She had a pack in her handbag, and fumbled for them in the darkness, stumbling on to the landing. Oliver was standing framed in the light from the bathroom. He had removed his shirt, his jeans moulded to the muscled length of his legs. A prickly awareness stirred the hairs on the back of her neck and in a daze Laurel handed him the tablets. Their fingers touched. Oliver swore shocking her with his vehemence.

'For Pete's sake, Laurel,' he muttered thickly, 'If it was experience you wanted, why the hell didn't you come to me?'

And then his mouth was closing over hers, hotly, druggingly, while his fingers moved impatiently against the buttons of her nightshirt, pushing it aside to reveal the fragile bones of her shoulders.

If she had thought she had experienced desire before, it was nothing compared with the torrent of feeling that raced through her now. The sensuous play of Oliver's fingers against her skin unlocked a door she had never guessed existed. She clung to him while his mouth burned against hers, clinging to him when he released her.

In the darkness it seemed to her that there was pain in his eyes as he looked at her, and then he said simply, 'I knew this afternoon I couldn't stay here with you tonight and not do this,' and then she was back in his arms, and he was carrying her to his bedroom—his bed, and she simply didn't care what she might be betraying to him in the feverish way she clung to his arms.

His hands on her body felt so right, she couldn't imagine how she could ever not have wanted them. They stroked a pathway along her collarbone and feathered down her spine, while she scattered feverish kisses against his throat.

When he tugged away her nightshirt she sighed with pleasure to feel the heat of his skin grazing the fullness of her breasts.

He raised himself slightly away from her, studying her body in the shadowy moonlight, one hand resting possessively on her thigh, the lazy movement of his thumb against the sensitive skin making her shiver with pleasure as she reached up towards him.

'Ask me again if I'm hungry, Laurel,' he murmured throatily. 'Or shall I simply show you?'

She felt his lips touch the pulse throbbing in her neck and then move downwards, exploring the delicacy of her skin. Nerves quivered in shocked pleasure at the intimacy of his touch, the sheer sensuality of his lovemaking as he explored and aroused every inch of her trembling body.

She cried out wildly with pleasure when his tongue touched the aroused peaks of her breasts, arching beneath him in complete abandonment in the desire he was invoking.

And he wanted her too. His jeans were discarded along with her nightshirt, the hesitant brush of her fingertips against his body bringing forth a muttered imprecation, evidence of his arousal apparent as he pulled her against him and her body responded joyously to the silken meshing of their skins.

Laurel wanted to kiss and touch him as he had done her, and she pressed her lips to his skin, feeling the tension in his muscles, and thinking she had done something wrong, until he groaned and moved convulsively tilting her head back so that he could plunder her mouth, his heart thudding heavily against her.

It was only when he parted her thighs and covered her with his body that fear suddenly intruded; a black stark fear that had its roots in the past, stiffening her body, making her cry out in fear and panic, until she realised that it wasn't Bill Trenchard who held her but Oliver, and then she sobbed his name, shivering with the remembered horror of the past, while he held and watched her, smoothing the tangled hair off her face.

'You thought I was Trenchard, didn't you?' he asked her huskily. 'My word, Laurel, what are you trying to do to me? What about Chas? Did you think he w. . . .?'

'You're wrong about Chas,' she told him. 'It wasn't like you think at all. We quarrelled on the way home and he left me. I had to walk, and I fell asleep. I . . . we didn't make love!'

She started to cry, slowly and helplessly,

knowing that he wouldn't believe her, but incredibly it seemed that he did.

'I would never have let him make love to me,' she told him through her tears. 'I had no idea. . . .'

'Which is why I spent half last night looking for you . . . which is right now why you should be in your own bed and not mine. One day, Laurel,' he told her, cupping her face, 'you're going to meet a man who's going to make you forget Trenchard—forget everything but your own need for him.'

She longed to say that she already had, but of course, Oliver didn't want her love. She wouldn't be here in his bed now if he hadn't been drinking, she was sure of that.

'What would you say now, if I asked you to stay with me?' he murmured, watching her.

Her heart gave a frightened bound. If he did could she resist him? She already knew the answer.

'I. . . .'

'It's all right,' he told her wryly, 'I'm not going to. You felt something, though, tonight, Laurel, you can't deny that, and I suppose that in itself is a breakthrough.'

In his experiment, he meant, of course. Misery and despair washed over her. She was playing with fire and she was going to get burned—badly. She loved Oliver, but he didn't love her, and she would be a fool to herself if she stayed with him even a minute longer, feeling as vulnerable as she did right now.

'I think I'd better go,' she told him woodenly. 'I. . . .'

'You were carried away in the heat of the moment. I know,' he told her dryly. 'Perhaps now you'll realise why I was so concerned when I thought you were with young Chas. It was plain that he wanted to go to bed with you from the moment he set eyes on you.'

Again Laurel thought she saw a flash of pain in his eyes, although it was gone too quickly for her to be sure.

As she moved away from him a shaft of moonlight touched his body, and she was flooded with a weakening desire to touch him, to beg him to make love to her, but if she did that he would know how she felt, and that was something she could not bear.

'For Pete's sake go if you're going, Laurel,' he told her hardily, hurting her with his indifference. 'I want some sleep even if you don't.'

And then he startled her by reaching for her nightshirt and buttoning her into it as though she were a child, although there was nothing childish about the way she felt as he anointed each breast with a lingering kiss before fastening the top few buttons.

Sleep! It had never been farther out of reach, because no matter how exhausted her body might be it couldn't forget the warm intimacy of Oliver's or stop longing for a return to the intimacy they had shared. Mental images of the masculine perfection of his body tormented her every time she closed her eyes.

CHAPTER NINE

THERE was no sign of Oliver when Laurel went downstairs. He came in just as she was waiting for the percolater—through the back door, his hair still damp, and his shirt open at the throat. For a moment she could only stare at him, remembering how last night . . . and then a rich tide of colour swept over her.

Oliver smiled a little quizzically, pulling up a chair and sitting down helping himself to some breakfast.

Of course her naïveté must seem amusing to him; what had to her been a momentous, world-shattering occurrence had to him simply been an experiment, a probe into her reactions.

She turned away abruptly and busied herself with the coffee, hoping that he hadn't seen how affected she was by him.

She heard the scrape of his chair as it was pushed back and then he was next to her, turning her to face him.

'Laurel, what happened last night is nothing you have to be ashamed of. I know how you must feel . . . at least I can guess how you must feel,' he corrected, 'especially in view of what I said to you yesterday morning. I couldn't have been more wrong about that, could I?' he probed with a gentleness that made her want to cry. 'I was a brute to you, and should have seen that. . . .'

'I was suffering from exhaustion because of my long walk and not. . . .'

'. . . because you had spent the night in Chas's

arms. What I'd like to know is what that young fool thought he was about, implying that you were with him.' His face hardened and for a moment Laurel barely recognised him. 'When I thīnk what might have happened to you. . . .!'

'He was very angry when. . . .'

'When you refused to let him make love to you?' Oliver intercepted. 'I can imagine.' His smile was mockingly wry as though he too could remember what it was like to know the frustration of thwarted desire. 'And not knowing your circumstances, he probably thought you'd simply been stringing him along. Even so, his behaviour was barely excusable in an eighteen-year-old; he should never have left you like that, and he can think himself lucky that I didn't find out until he was beyond my reach!' He looked at her when Laurel laughed huskily, and then grimaced. 'I suppose you're thinking that after last night I have scant excuse for criticising someone else's standards. About last night, Laurel. . . .'

He released her and walked away, hand resting on his hips as he stared through the window, his back towards her. 'I want to talk to you about it, to explain that. . . .'

'No, there's really no need. I do understand,' Laurel rushed in nervously. 'These things happen, and I suppose because of the way things were . . . with you knowing about my . . . my past, and me. . . .' 'loving you,' she had been about to say, but broke off in time and instead substituted, 'knowing you from then, it was sort of inevitable.'

'I'm glad that you can take it so philosophically!'

He still hadn't turned to face her, and Laurel wasn't sure if she liked the cool mockery of his voice. It seemed to hint at a sheathed anger that could prove lethal if it was ever allowed to escape, although she couldn't understand what she had done to arouse it. Could he have wanted her to admit that she knew why he had made love to her?

She began to feel faintly sick. Had he already noted down her reactions to his lovemaking, stored them away somewhere to use in his book? She berated herself for not having the courage to demand angrily that he stopped using her, but she couldn't face the inevitable pain of seeing the amused contempt in his eyes when she did so. What right had she to feel hurt or betrayed? Oliver had never for one moment professed to feel any emotion for her. No one had forced her to lie wantonly in his arms, inviting the silken caress of his skin against hers—far from it. She might have been repressed and virginal, but she wasn't a fool; she did know that men were capable of purely physical desire.

'I haven't told you have I,' Oliver continued abruptly, 'But I have to go to Nice first thing tomorrow morning—Alone,' he added turning towards her. 'I'll be gone all day.'

'You'll want to give me plenty of dictation today then,' Laurel marvelled at her ability to keep her voice normal and level when inside she was aching with pain. Why was he going to Nice? To see a woman? It was a question she couldn't ask, but Oliver was a man who would never be short of female companionship, and she guessed that she was a poor substitute for the women he normally consorted with.

'I don't think so. I'm still very much at the "thinking" stage, and you're proving an even greater distraction than I feared,' he told her. 'Tape machines are far less troublesome.'

She managed a smile, as though she thought he

was joking, but inwardly she was a mass of anguish.

It was several minutes before he spoke again, putting down the cup of coffee she had poured to ask shockingly, 'Laurel, last night—was it entirely my imagination, or did you derive as much pleasure from our . . . intimacy, as it seemed?'

Her cheeks were on fire. How could he sit there so calmly discussing what had happened as though he were dissecting a chapter of one of his books?

'I'm not sure what you mean,' she hedged at last. 'I. . . .'

'What I mean,' he explained patiently, getting up and turning to face her, 'is were you merely acting when you responded to me as you did, or. . . .'

A confusion of thoughts jostled through her mind. Should she lie and say she had been pretending? But what if he knew she was lying, would he then guess the reason why she had lied?

'I wasn't acting,' she managed at last. 'But. . . .'

'But I mustn't misinterpret what you did feel? Don't worry, Laurel. I'm well aware of the potency of physical desire. I'm pleased that you've discovered it too, because it helps to absolve me from a sin that's weighed heavily on my conscience, even if it has turned out to be a viciously sharp double-edged sword,' he said cryptically. 'You must never be ashamed of your sexuality,' he added frankly, 'and never abuse it. It's a gift—to you and to your lover. I would hate you to have suffered all these years believing yourself to be frigid, only to go completely in the opposite direction. A woman who values herself cherishes her body, bestowing it as a gift; the supreme gift when desire is matched by love. What I'm trying to say,' he added ruefully, 'and not very well, it seems, is that for all this is a permissive age, you have a fragility and sensitivity that could be all too easily crushed by careless fingers. I sound like a Victorian papa trying to warn his precious daughter against the perils of the flesh!'

'But you aren't my father ... and I'm already well aware of them,' Laurel reminded him unevenly. 'I learned them young, remember?'

For a moment a tinge of red seeped under his skin, making her feel that she had dealt him a mortal blow. Tension stretched between them like a fine wire, and suddenly she could bear it no longer. With a small cry she ran from the room, leaving him staring after her.

Let him think whatever he wanted, she thought childishly an hour later, arms wrapped round her hunched knees as she stared out across the countryside. Did he still think she was an impressionable twelve-year-old? Was that still how he saw her? Not as a woman, but as a child?

The tension between them seemed to thicken as the day wore on. Oliver was in a strange mood, bitingly sarcastic one moment and silent the next. Nothing Laurel did was right, and on several occasions his cutting comments brought her close to tears, all the more so because she knew his barbs weren't justified.

Did he suspect how she felt about him? Did he think she had some sort of silly crush on him and he was using this method of stamping it out? If only that were possible!

Laurel didn't want much dinner. It was Oliver's turn to make it, and his mouth tightened ominously when he saw how much of the lasagne he had made she had left. Her listless, 'I'm not very hungry,' brought only a further tightening of his mouth, and she couldn't help noticing the generous measure of whisky he poured for himself after dinner, barely doing more than splashing it with water, before tossing it down his throat.

She remembered how her stepfather used to return home the worse for drink.

'There's no need to look like that. I can drink a good deal more than this without showing any ill effects,' Oliver snapped at her, when her expression unwittingly betrayed her. 'Or are you thinking that this,' he tapped his whisky glass, 'might mean a repetition of last night? You've got a lot to learn, my dear,' he sneered, shocking her with his bitterness. 'When a man has to bolster himself with drink before he can enter a woman's bed, it's rarely an exercise he wants to repeat!'

He strode across the living room and selected a record which he placed on the hi-fi, but in place of the soothing strains Laurel had expected to hear, the sounds that filled the room were aggressive and warring.

'To match the mood,' Oliver taunted when she grimaced faintly. 'But if you don't care for it. . . .'

'I think I'll have an early night—I'm tired.' Her voice faltered and she half expected some blistering sardonic retort, but none was forthcoming. When she lifted her head, Oliver was staring grimly into the glass he was slowly rotating between his hands.

There was a book on the chair, and Laurel picked it up blindly. She wasn't really that tired, and it would be something to read; something to help her sleep and perhaps banish the torturing memories that seemed to spring up like a sowing of dragon's teeth, tormenting her with what might have been.

It was only when she had bathed and gone to bed that she realised the book was one of those Oliver had purchased in Arles. It was in English, written by a psychiatrist with a long string of letters after his name, and out of curiosity she started to thumb through it, her expression slowly changing as she realised it was a work dealing almost exclusively with problems such as those she herself had experienced; case histories in the main, many of them almost identical to her own. Children, pre-adolescent or just adolescent, who had experienced some sort of mental scarring due to the sexual overtones of those in authority over them. Many of the cases dealt with incest, some with actual rape, and Laurel was shivering like someone suffering from palsy by the time she had finished. And she had to finish it; even though almost every page, every word, brought back a deluge of memories, her eyes remained riveted to the book. She read how Dr Ealies considered that the first step back to normality for sufferers in these cases was the ability to form a relationship based on trust with a member of the opposite sex; how young adolescents who suffered this particularly harmful adult perversion had to be taught to re-code their senses to experience pleasure where before they had experienced fear, pain and humiliation. The more she read the more Laurel realised how fortunate she had been that her case had been relatively mild; and how for her the ability to trust had not been completely destroyed, otherwise she would never have been able to confide in Oliver in the first place. She also felt with renewed conviction that the hatred she had professed to feel for him had been the result of her belief that he had deliberately violated that trust.

Oliver could only have bought this book

because of her; because he wanted to gain a deeper insight into how her mind worked, which surely must be a plain indication that he was, as she had suspected, using her, or parts of her, with the intention of learning all he could about her so that he could re-create her in his book. When she finally closed the book, Laurel felt as though she had finally emerged from the tunnel that had closed round her when Bill Trenchard became her stepfather. She would have loved Oliver no matter when they met or where, she knew now, because what she felt for him was a woman's love for a man.

She fell asleep at last, but the book had re-awakened memories she had deliberately subdued over the years, and now they came flooding back; her stepfather, threatening to send her away; touching her; filling her with fury and fear. In her nightmare she relived again the scene that had culminated in the trial—her stepfather pinning her to the floor, his sour breath in her face, her terror when his hands touched her naked skin.

A scream bubbled in her throat, her threshing body dislodging the bedclothes, as scream after scream tore at her throat. It was the bedroom door crashing open that broke the horror. Oliver's hands on her body were soothing, as she opened her eyes and saw him watching her with concern in his eyes.

'Laurel! I thought you were being murdered at the very least,' he said with a wry attempt at humour.

Still drugged with the terror of her dream, Laurel shuddered, her eyes huge and staring in her pale face.

From the floor Oliver rescued the book she had borrowed.

'I read it,' she told him huskily. 'It brought it all back ... Bill ... the night ... the night. ...'

'He tried to rape you? I was in court, Laurel,' he told her, 'I heard it all, but it's over now. It was just a nightmare—unpleasant, as I should know, I've had my fair share in my time.' She barely noticed the oddly brooding quality of his words.

Still caught up in the horror of her nightmare, Laurel could only tremble and stare at him, flinching as he put out a hand to touch her arm, grey eyes replaced by hot brown ones; Oliver's strong compassionate features with Bill's greedily lustful ones.

She shrank away from him, murmuring breathless protests, her eyes dilated with the emotion of what she was reliving.

'Laurel!'

The mists cleared and her eyes focused properly. 'Oh, Oliver!' Her voice trembled and she flung herself into his arms. 'It was so awful ... so real,' she told him huskily as his arms closed round her, her head rested on his shoulder, a sense of wellbeing and homecoming washing over her. Seconds ticked by and a drowsy lassitude replaced her earlier terror. The warm, male scent of Oliver's skin tantalised her nostrils, and suddenly simply being held by him wasn't enough.

'Laurel? Laurel, are you all right now?'

Sensing his withdrawal, her fingers curled into the open lapels of his shirt, her plaintive, 'Don't leave me, Oliver, please! I'm frightened I might start dreaming again,' drawing his brows together in a frown.

'What are you suggesting?' he asked her cynically. 'That we spend the entire night like this?'

Her pulses leapt at the thought, and an aching yearning spread through her body.

'Laurel. . . .'

'Oliver, don't leave me, please!' she pleaded, gripping him tighter. 'Please!'

His fingers were already on her wrists, as though he intended to push her away forcibly, and then suddenly his expression changed, his thumbs stroking sensuously over the sensitive inner flesh of her wrists. A sighing breath was wrenched from her, and Oliver's face contorted as he muttered thickly, 'Oh heavens!' and Laurel didn't know if it was an imprecation or a prayer, as his mouth closed on hers with a compulsive hunger that obliterated for all time any image of Bill Trenchard. This was Oliver, and every nerve ending in her body knew it and welcomed him. His lips moved over hers with growing insistence, as though, incredibly, he felt the same wild hunger that tore at her. Amazingly, unbelievably, she was free; and she felt dizzy, lightheaded with the knowledge.

'Laurel, Laurel.' He muttered her name into her throat, arching it with the pressure of his mouth, stroking the quivering flesh with his tongue, drawing sensual shudders of pleasure from her.

It was like being caught in a maelstrom where no past or future existed, only a vast wave now that encompassed only them and the tight thread of tension that had been there all day, culminating in the explosion of need that burst like a fireball between them.

Her fingers tightened into his hair, loving the feel of his scalp, the texture of his hair, and her mouth parted willingly for the heated invasion of his.

She shivered with anticipation as his hands stroked over her body, with a delicacy that tantalised, her breath trapped in her lungs, desiring him as much as he seemed to desire her.

There was no thought in her head of holding back; her fingers tugged experimentally at the buttons on his shirt, her tongue touching her lip as she concentrated all her attention on the hair-roughened expanse of chest she was slowly revealing; lost in rapt contemplation of his maleness, her fingers moving with undisguised pleasure over the muscular wall of his chest.

'Laurel!' His hoarse groan sent a frisson of answering need along her sensitised nerves, as her lips moved slowly over his skin, following the path of her fingers.

Wholly absorbed in the pleasure of touching him, she forgot that he didn't love her, and knew only of their mutual need.

The protest that jerked past his lips as her fingers trailed tantalisingly across his stomach resting on the buckle of his jeans provoked an elemental thrill of power. His hands stroked her breasts, and she moaned softly with fresh delight, impatient for the hard warmth of his body against hers.

He paused, removing his jeans with fingers that trembled visibly, and Laurel responded eagerly to the growing urgency of his touch.

His lips playing erotically with the firm tautness of her nipples made her moan with an aching pleasure that began somewhere deep inside her and spread to every nerve. She was drowning, lost in a stomach-clenching excitement that drove her on with no thought of the consequences. Oliver's hard masculinity against her brought her to a fresh peak of frenzied pleasure, and her body writhed instinctively beneath his, welcoming his intimate caresses without shame or restraint.

'Laurel, is this really you?' Oliver muttered against her throat. 'I can hardly believe it. Are you really free at last? No more hang-ups, no more. . . .'

Laurel stiffened in his arms. Why, oh, why had he had to remind her? If only he had simply gone on making love to her, by now she might be experiencing his complete possession instead of lying here knowing that what to her had been the culmination of her love was to him nothing more than therapy.

'Yes, I'm free,' she said dully, pulling away from him. 'There's no need to go any further, Oliver. The experiment is over.'

'Experiment?' She had his full attention now. 'What the hell are you talking about?' He sat up, a shadowy, alien outline watching her.

'You know what I mean. You were using me, monitoring me so that you could use me in your book. I guessed it almost from the first—the way you questioned me about the past; everything.'

'Laurel, that simply isn't. . . .' He broke off, moving angrily and dislodging the pile of articles she had brought upstairs and her notebook. 'What the. . . .?' He frowned, then snapped on the bedside lamp, flooding the room with light. 'What are you doing with these?' he asked her, frowning over the articles, 'and this? What is it?' He picked up the notebook and it fell open. He read a few lines and then looked at her.

Laurel shrivelled under that look, combined of a combustible anger and ice-cold contempt.

'My word,' he breathed emotively, quickly reading down the rest of the page, 'and you had the gall to accuse me! What the devil is this?'

'Oliver, I can explain. . . .' Desperately she reached for the notebook, but he held her off, quickly flipping through some of the pages, his expression hardening with every word.

'So,' he said in the silence that followed, 'now we have the truth. You came here with me with the deliberate intention of somehow discrediting me. Don't even bother trying to deny it, Laurel. It's all here, written down by you.'

What could she say? That it was true that she had written those things, felt them even, but she had been muddled and confused then by her own motives, had not fully understood how she had felt. She couldn't confess the truth to him—not now.

'Damn!' he swore softly, 'and to think I actually. ally. ... What a pity you're so wrapped up in your bigoted prejudices of the past, otherwise you might have realised there was a better weapon to hand.' His lip curled as he stared down at her. 'Publish and be damned, Laurel,' he breathed bitterly. 'I was mistaken about you after all—pity!'

He had gone before she had the presence of mind to remind him that his own actions scarcely bore looking into, and she was left feeling as though she had committed some unpardonable sin. She hated him thinking that she had actually intended to injure him in some way, but how could she have told him the truth? If only she had destroyed that notebook!

When she got up in the morning Oliver had gone to Nice.

She spent an hour pacing the floor, wondering how she could continue working for him, and then the sound of a car brought her to the window, a surprised smile breaking through her frown as she recognised Elizabeth's Range Rover.

'I'm afraid Oliver is in Nice,' she told her, 'and he won't be back until tomorrow.'

'We're only stopping briefly—we won't wait for him. We're rushing back because an aunt of my husband's has suddenly been taken ill.'

While Laurel sympathised the children poured out of the car. She could make a meal for them, Laurel offered.

'I hoped to get the opportunity to have a word with you,' Elizabeth confided when the children went down to the pool. 'I'm dreadfully sorry about what happened with Chas. He admitted the truth to Rick in Marbella.'

'It doesn't really matter,' Laurel assured her. A plan was forming in her mind. Could she beg a lift home with Elizabeth?

Oliver would scarcely want her to stay now, and if she did how long would it be before she embarrassed them both by betraying her feelings.

'Actually,' she began hesitantly, 'I was wondering if I could possibly beg a ride back to England with you?'

Elizabeth frowned. 'That's a sudden decision, isn't it? Does Oliver know?'

'No, but I don't think he'll mind.' Laurel pulled a face. 'We had a row, and to be honest with you, I think it's best that I leave now.'

'For you or for him?' Elizabeth asked dryly. 'What about his book?'

'Oh, I think he's got everything he needed from me for that now,' Laurel told her bitterly. 'No doubt his book will be another runaway best-seller, although I won't be buying it.'

'I'm afraid you've lost me,' Elizabeth told her calmly. 'Come and sit down and tell me all about it.'

Normally Laurel wouldn't have dreamed of confiding in anyone else, but her emotions were so raw from the quarrel with Oliver that it was a relief to unburden herself.

Elizabeth frowned occasionally, but didn't interrupt as Laurel told her of her suspicions.

'You're wrong, I'm sure of it,' she announced positively when Laurel had finished. 'Oliver would never do that. Oh, I can understand why you might think that he was using you, but I know him, Laurel. I know how terribly he suffered when he realised how he had misjudged you. He searched high and low for you. He doesn't confide in me, but if you want my opinion I believe if anything he was simply trying to help you, Laurel.

'I can imagine the trauma you must have suffered through your stepfather—I'm not saying Oliver was right in what he did, but I do believe his motives were completely altruistic. Of course, there is another explanation.' She shot a look at Laurel. 'He could be in love with you!'

Laurel stared at her, the breath leaving her lungs in a painful gasp. 'No.' She shook her head vehemently. 'No, he isn't.'

'But you love him,' Elizabeth submitted shrewdly, 'and that's why you want to leave. Oh, my dear, isn't it worth staying and talking the whole thing through with him?'

'I'd really rather not. If you feel you can't give me a lift, I suppose I could always get a taxi to Arles, and then. . . .'

'If you're really determined of course you must come with us, although I shudder to think what Oliver will say to me when he discovers how you escaped!'

Something told Laurel that Elizabeth could be more than a match for her formidable brother when she chose, but she didn't say so. Overlying her relief at the thought of escape was a growing sense of loss. She would never see Oliver again;

how could she bear it? Could she bear the alternative?

She refused to look behind them as the Range Rover pulled away from the farmhouse. She had left Oliver a note explaining that in view of what had happened she thought it best that she leave. There was no need to say any more, and although Elizabeth gave her one or two thoughtful glances as they drove north she asked no more questions and proffered no advice.

Laurel was sorry to say goodbye to her when they eventually parted. In other circumstances they could have become friends.

CHAPTER TEN

ANOTHER week over, thank goodness, Laurel reflected as she turned the key in the lock of her flat. She had only been in it six weeks—she had got it just after she returned from Italy where she had been working for most of the summer. Taking on temporary work with the agency when she returned from Arles had been a brainwave—all those interesting stints at various offices and then a summer job working as an extra secretary, to a film producer, filming in Italy. The job had only been temporary, but very exhilarating. She could have gone out with a different male almost every night had she chosen to do so, but somehow, although she had lost her old reticence with men, she had no desire to encourage any of them in a closer relationship than mere friendship.

Her skin was still tanned from the Italian sun. She had lost the pinched, haggard look she had worn for so long, her body was supple and sleek.

Her latest job had been working in a busy office, but it was over now, and the agency had warned her that with the winter months approaching temporary work might become harder to come by. She was toying with the idea of writing to her former employers to enquire if they had any vacancies, although she wasn't sure how Mr Marshall would find the new Laurel.

Not that she had really changed, she had merely come out of her shell, developed the poise and self-confidence she had previously lacked. These days she wore her hair loose and glossy, her face was discreetly but attractively made up, her clothes were sleekly smart, but there was still something missing from her life.

Initially, she had gone out with other men, hoping against hope that she might after all have been mistaken; that her love for Oliver might only have been a crush, but when they kissed her, it was simply a kiss, sometimes pleasurable, sometimes not, but never evoking the response Oliver's kisses had.

She let herself into her flat with a sigh of relief. She had been invited to a party tonight, but she wasn't really in the mood. She decided that she would stay in instead.

Half an hour later she was sitting in front of the television, eating the meal she had prepared, idly watching the chat show that was on.

The host was talking to one of his guests, and Laurel listened halfheartedly, tensing suddenly as he turned back to the camera and announced, 'And now my next guest really needs no introduction—his work speaks for itself. Ladies and gentlemen, the celebrated winner of this year's Maundale Prize, Oliver Savage, or Jonathan Graves, as his public know him better.'

Laurel was transfixed, her meal forgotten as her eyes moved hungrily over the familiar features. Oliver was wearing a formal suit, looking impossibly handsome, and so the show's female guest seemed to think as well, Laurel thought jealously, watching the way she reached over to touch his arm, smiling warmly into his eyes.

She was so engrossed in Oliver himself that she missed the first few questions. He looked drawn somehow, but that might simply be the effect of appearing on television; his face seemed more sharply defined.

'And now perhaps you'd like to tell us something about your new book,' the host prompted, but Oliver shook his head.

'I can't describe it in a handful of words. All I will say is that it's something I had to write; needed to write.'

'You make it sound like a form of therapy,' Laurel heard the chat show host say curiously.

'If it was it didn't work,' was Oliver's wry response.

The interview lasted a few minutes longer and then the cameras switched to another guest, but Laurel remained glued in front of the set for the remainder of the programme, hoping for another glimpse of Oliver.

Nothing had changed; if anything seeing him simply re-affirmed what she already knew—that she loved him and always would.

She received a pleasant but disappointing response to her letter to her old employers. There were no vacancies just at the moment, and in desperation she accepted a part-time job from the agency, working in a large store.

She was on her way back to the office one lunchtime when she noticed that the book department was assembling a new display.

'It's for the new Jonathan Graves,' the girl informed her. 'I'm certainly going to buy it. Did you see him on television the other week? He's gorgeous!'

Laurel told herself that it would be stupid to pile on the agony by reading his book, but nevertheless, she found herself walking towards the book department several days later, on her way to lunch. It was very busy, a crowd of people thronging round the stand where she had seen

Oliver's book. It was only as she approached that Laurel realised the reason why.

Oliver was there in person, signing copies of the book!

Her stomach churned in disbelief, the blood rushing to her head as she stood and stared.

He couldn't possible have known she was there, of course, and yet there was an instant when he lifted his head and seemed to stare right at her, their eyes meeting.

Impossible that he could have seen her, Laurel decided as she hurried away; she doubted that he even remembered her except as an interesting subject. They hadn't even parted as friends, thanks to her stupidity over her 'revenge'. How childishly immature that seemed now!

Christmas approached and Laurel forced herself to do all the seasonal things. She had friends she could spend it with now—young people like herself living alone in London—but the idea had little appeal. She toyed with the idea of going away. The agency had a job on offer as a cook at a chalet in Gstaad, but then she read in the gossip columns that Oliver was spending Christmas in Switzerland, and she declined, fearing, ridiculously, that she might meet him. If she did, she had no faith in her ability not to betray herself to him, and she didn't want to add that stupidity to all her others.

The week before Christmas she received a card with a Dorset postmark. It had been forwarded to her by Marshalls. Puzzled, she opened it, astounded to discover that it was from Oliver's sister. Presumably she had learned from Oliver that she used to work at Marshalls and had assumed that she had gone back to work there. If it hadn't been for the coincidence of her trying to get a job there she would never have received the card, Laurel reflected, because they wouldn't have known her address.

As she opened it a folded note fell out.

It was a brief but warm invitation for her to visit them over the New Year when, Elizabeth explained, they normally had a large informal party.

'You have no need to worry about bumping into Oliver,' she had written. 'He's away in Switzerland, but I should very much like to see you again.'

And she would like to see her, Laurel admitted, if only to hear Oliver's name mentioned. How compulsively unfair to themselves those in love are, she reflected as she re-read the note. She knew that it would be safer and wiser to refuse, and yet she felt an urgent need to accept, to be close to those Oliver was close to.

She was a fool if she accepted, she told herself, but that didn't stop her sitting down and replying that she would be delighted to spend the weekend with them.

She spent the next week alternating between excitement and depression. Of course she wouldn't be seeing Oliver, but she would hear all those little things her heart craved; little intimate family details that would flesh out the bare scraps she read in the press.

She decided to drive down. Christmas had been mild and damp—and very lonely, although she was loath to admit that even to herself. She had bought a new dress for the party, plain black crêpe that fitted her like a glove, swirling out into a softly full skirt cut on the bias, and pintucked demurely down the bodice. It had been far more expensive than she had expected, but it was undoubtedly 'her', and because she hoped that if

Elizabeth did ever mention her visit to Oliver, it would be in flattering terms, she bought it and prayed that she would soon find a permanent job.

Elizabeth had telephoned her during the week, giving her explicit instructions as to how to find them.

'The house is a barn,' she confided blithely. 'My husband's family have owned it for years, and there are times when it drives me mad, but there are others when I'm overwhelmed by a ridiculous sentimentality towards it. I'm so pleased you're coming,' she added flatteringly. 'We're all looking forward to seeing you tremendously.'

The drive down to Dorset was uneventful. Laurel stopped on the way to have a quick lunch at a roadside pub. A group of men by the bar eyed her admiringly, and although she ignored them she felt none of the terrified revulsion their appreciation would once have caused. She had Oliver to thank for that, of course.

It was mid-afternoon when she eventually drew up outside the weathered, rambling stone building Elizabeth had described to her.

The twins came flying out as though they had been expecting her, their voices disconcertingly on the verge of breaking.

Rick was not far behind, blushing faintly as he took her case. In half a dozen or so years' time he would be very like Oliver, but right now he was still very much a boy.

'Come on in,' Elizabeth told her, emerging from the house and welcoming her with a hug. 'Graham has been called out on an urgent case—a baby eager to make its arrival before the year goes out!'

She led the way into a rectangular-shaped hall cluttered with myriad pairs of wellingtons, coats and dog leads.

'It may be chaos, but it's home.' Elizabeth grinned. 'Actually it's not normally quite as bad as this, it's just that Mrs Simmonds our invaluable housekeeper is away at the moment.'

'Then you must let me do what I can to help,' Laurel told her. 'Are you expecting other guests?'

The twins looked puzzled, and seemed about to say something but Elizabeth said quickly, 'Er . . . I'm not quite sure yet. Look, let me take you up to your room, and then we'll have a cup of tea. Jane is staying with a friend at the moment—you know what girls of that age are, they're practically inseparable at the moment, and of course she couldn't wait to show her her new bike. I only hope we've done the right thing. The roads round here are relatively quiet, but even so . . . We're sending her on one of these courses just to make sure she knows what she's doing. It won't do any harm.'

She ushered Laurel into a pretty, floral-decorated bedroom. 'This house was originally the vicarage,' she told Laurel. 'My husband's great-grandfather was the vicar here, and then eventually he bought it from the Church and it's been in my husband's family ever since.'

'It's lovely,' Laurel assured her truthfully, looking out of the window at the bare winter landscape.

'It has its moments,' Elizabeth agreed. 'I'll leave you to unpack and then we can catch up on one another's gossip over a cup of tea. It's just family for dinner this evening.'

'You must have an awful lot on your hands with the party to prepare for,' Laurel guessed. 'Anything I can do to help?'

'Er . . . well, actually everything's pretty much under control, even though it doesn't look it. We tend to take things fairly casually down here; there isn't any of the pomp and circumstance of a London party.'

When Laurel had unpacked she went downstairs and found her hostess alone in the comfortable chintzy living room.

'Just in time,' Elizabeth smiled, indicating the teapot. 'Now come and sit down and tell me what you've been doing with yourself. You've been an extremely elusive creature to find.'

'I've been working abroad, doing temporary work,' Laurel told her, accepting a cup of tea, and absently stroking the smooth head of the golden retriever who had padded to her side. 'Exhausting but very invigorating. I enjoyed it.'

'You've emerged from your chrysalis with a vengeance,' Elizabeth commented. 'Oliver will be pleased. He's been worried about you.'

'There was no need.' Laurel bent her head over her teacup so that Elizabeth couldn't see her expression. Merely hearing his name sent shafts of mingled anguish and delight stabbing through her, traitorous memories undermining all her resolutions to put him out of her mind.

'Try convincing him of that,' Elizabeth said dryly. 'He wasn't very pleased with me when he discovered I'd been a party to your moonlight flit!'

How weak she was to feel a surge of primitive delight at this disclosure! To punish herself she said briefly, 'I'm sorry if my abrupt departure meant that he couldn't do any more field research, but. . . .'

'You'd fallen in love with him and had to get away,' Elizabeth supplemented gently, reminding her of their previous conversation. 'Perhaps in some ways it was inevitable.'

'Because of the past?' Laurel asked her,

surprised to discover how free of embarrassment and constraint she felt at talking so frankly. 'I did think that myself for a while; I even hoped that perhaps what I felt for him was a sort of delayed reaction crush—the first time I met him, just after the trial, I felt instantly drawn to him. He seemed so sympathetic, so understanding. It came as a tremendous blow to discover that he'd simply been using me—almost as great a blow in some ways as what had gone before. For years I harboured bitter feelings towards him, I suppose I transferred the hate I felt towards my stepfather on to Oliver, but when I met him again, when he explained to me why he had done what he did, and how he felt when he discovered that he'd been wrong, I realised I'd been hating a character who existed only in my own mind. The real Oliver was quite different, and I found myself falling in love with him.'

'It never occurred to you that the situation could be mutual?' Elizabeth asked her.

Laurel shook her head. 'How could it be? Oh, I know he felt a certain amount of pity for me; but basically as far as he was concerned I was just an interesting subject to be studied and used.'

'But he made love to you,' Elizabeth reminded her.

'If you can call it that. As I said before, I think he was simply trying to discover if it was possible to break through the fear encasing me. There was nothing really personal in it. It was an experiment; a series of experiments.'

'Have you read his new book?'

Laurel shook her head. 'I was going to buy it, and then I changed my mind. He's in Switzerland at the moment, I believe?'

She hated herself for asking the question, but

talking about the past had weakened her resolve
not to spend the weekend drowning in nostalgia
and pain.

'He spent Christmas there,' Elizabeth agreed, 'I
can hear a car,' she told Laurel. 'I think it will be
Graham.' She stood up, and Laurel envied her the
soft smile of anticipation curving her mouth as she
looked out of the window. It must be wonderful to
still feel pleasure in someone's company after so
many years of marriage. Would she herself ever
marry? Somehow she doubted it.

Graham Turner turned out to be every bit as
pleasant as his wife, a placid humorous man.
Laurel could well imagine that he made a perfect
foil for Elizabeth's more effervescent personality.

'Twins, would you believe it,' he told her in
response to her query about his patient. 'Derek is
as pleased as punch, but a bit poleaxed, and Moira
came through the whole thing splendidly. One of
the bonuses of being a doctor,' he told Laurel with
a smile. 'The miracle of witnessing the beginning
of a new life is something that never loses its
magic. What's for dinner?' he asked his wife
mundanely.

Elizabeth laughed and winked at Laurel. 'It does
wonders for the appetite as well, so it seems! It's
one of your favourites, as it so happens, beef
Wellington—which reminds me, I ought to be
doing something in the kitchen.'

Over dinner Laurel had more leisure to study
the family en masse, and she couldn't help feeling
a twinge of envy as she listened to their cheerful
banter. The twins were teasing Rick about his
latest girl-friend, their father interrupting them
whenever they got a little out of hand, all of them
including Laurel in the conversation in such a way
that she almost felt part of them.

After dinner she helped to load the dishwasher and enjoyed the lively discussion in the living room between the twins and their parents about the importance of education.

'Exhausting, aren't they?' Elizabeth announced when they left to go and play table tennis.

Laurel had been invited to join them but had declined. It had been a long day and she was beginning to feel tired.

'One of the bonuses of having such a large house is that at least we have plenty of room for hobbies. We've turned what used to be the cellars into a games room—marvellous for keeping them off the streets!'

Perhaps it was the fresh air, Laurel reflected the next morning, but she couldn't remember when she had last slept as well. A cold nose pushed impatiently at her elbow and she glanced down at the golden retriever grinning silently beside the bed, tail beating anxiously.

'Susie, you naughty girl!' she heard Elizabeth exclaiming from the door. 'I'm sorry about that, Laurel,' she apologised, coming in with a tray of tea, 'but Susie has appointed herself official looker-in on our guests, and she sneaked up here before I could stop her. She isn't really allowed upstairs.'

'It can't really be that time!' Laurel was appalled to discover that it was almost nine. What on earth must the Turners think of her?

'Don't worry about it. Actually, I'm afraid I have an apology to make to you. I'd completely forgotten when we invited you that I promised to go and see an old friend today. She and I were at school together and we normally visit them a couple of times a year. I could cancel it, but. . . .'

She looked so worried that Laurel said quickly, 'No, please don't do that, I promise you I can keep myself occupied for a few hours. Perhaps I could do something towards the party?'

'Er . . . yes . . . well, there's no need to worry about that, but if you're really sure you don't mind?'

As her friend lived in Bath, to make the visit worthwhile they would have to leave immediately after lunch, Elizabeth explained to Laurel.

Graham was going with her—one of his rare afternoons off, and Laurel decided she would spend part of the afternoon exploring the countryside, perhaps taking Susie with her for company. She had noticed an inviting footpath from her bedroom window, but when she mentioned this idea, Elizabeth looked almost horrified.

'Oh, no . . . that is . . . er. . . .'

'The weather forecast isn't looking too good,' Graham supplied for her. 'The temperature is dropping pretty quickly, and unless you've come properly equipped I wouldn't suggest a walk.'

Perhaps they were worried that she was too much of a city dweller to be trusted to go out walking on her own, Laurel reflected, but whatever the reason she had no wish to worry them, and so she said instead that she would find some way of entertaining herself.

What she had in mind was table tennis with the twins, but no sooner had their parents left than the boys announced that they had promised to meet some friends in the village.

Was it something about her? Laurel wondered humorously; at least Susie seemed to want her company.

Even Rick had deserted her; gone to see his girl-friend, the twins explained knowledgeably as they left.

And now there was one, Laurel thought as she wondered how best to spend the afternoon.

With the party in mind she decided to enjoy a long luxurious soak in the pretty bathroom off her bedroom, and then a proper manicure for her nails. It was a sybaritic, lazy way of spending the afternoon at least.

She had just emerged from the water, her body scented deliciously with her favourite perfume, when she heard a car outside the house. It was too early for it to be Graham and Elizabeth returning, and thinking it might be someone needing a doctor, Laurel hurriedly pulled on her towelling robe and ran downstairs.

She reached the door just as she heard a key in the lock. It turned, and Susie, who was whining excitedly, rushed towards the door as it swung open, her whole body quivering with pleasure.

'Down, Susie, you silly dog!'

The familiar voice held Laurel transfixed, her eyes widening in shocked recognition of Oliver's familiar figure. He seemed taller and broader in the narrow black pants and dark grey leather blouson, the collar turned up against the cold. His hair needed cutting, she noticed absently as he turned and she saw where it grew over the collar of his jacket. He seemed strangely unsurprised to see her, although something, some emotion she couldn't recognise, flickered in his eyes, as he gently pushed the dog away and said evenly, 'Hello, Laurel.'

'I thought you were in Switzerland!'

Her voice sounded thick and unsteady. She clung to the banister for support, not sure how much longer her trembling legs would support her

'I know,' he told her tersely. 'Let's get inside, shall we?'

He took her arm, and beneath the towelling she was acutely conscious of the strength of his fingers, darkly tanned against the white fabric.

'You've been very elusive,' he told her curtly as he closed the door behind them.

Her mouth had gone dry, and she moistened her lips nervously with the tip of her tongue, trembling uncertainly as she watched Oliver's eyes darken and narrow as he watched her.

'I . . . I didn't know you were looking for me.'

'Oh, come on, Laurel,' he drawled sardonically. 'You can do better than that! You knew damn well we had things to talk about.'

'If you mean what I wrote in my notebook,' she began uncertainly, 'it was a mistake—I realised that almost straight away. I did feel bitter about you at first, before I realised that . . . I would never have gone through with what I'd planned,' she finished nervously.

'So you don't hate me after all?' There was a curious thread of uncertainty in his voice, a look in his eyes that set her pulses racing madly.

She turned, glancing down at a table, startled to realise that a copy of his new book lay on it. She picked it up, disconcerted to find that he was watching her carefully.

'Have you read it yet?'

Laurel shook her head.

'I'd like you to, but not yet. First we have to talk. Why did you run away from me, Laurel? And not just once. That time in the bookshop, I tried to signal to you that I wanted to talk, but you disappeared.'

So he had seen her, and it hadn't been purely her imagination that he had been trying to communicate something to her.

'What about?' she managed evenly. 'I thought you'd concluded your experiment. You said you were going to turn me into a woman, didn't you, and. . . .'

'Experiment? Just what the hell are you talking about?' he demanded in a driven tone, his expression suddenly changing, as he muttered hoarsely, 'Oh, damn, Laurel, do you have to walk around half naked? How the hell am I supposed to concentrate on what I'm saying when all I can think about is the fact that you're wearing damn all underneath that robe, and how desperately I want to touch you. Oh, Laurel, if you knew how much I've wanted you these last months! It's been purgatory, but this is even worse. I love you,' he said thickly, 'and God forgive me, although I swore I'd never say it, never use emotional blackmail to get you back in my arms, I can't help myself, just as I can't help doing this. I love you, and it's tearing me apart,' he muttered savagely as he jerked her into his arms, burying his mouth hotly in hers, possessing it with a compulsive need that went far beyond anything she had experienced before.

It was several long, satisfying minutes, when she simply allowed what she was feeling to obliterate everything else, and responded feverishly to his nearness, savouring the crisp feel of his hair beneath her fingers, letting them trace the breadth of his shoulders as she slipped them beneath his jacket, before he released her.

'Laurel, you can't respond to me like that and not feel something,' he groaned at last, holding her away from her.

'Can't I?' She peeped demurely up at him from beneath downswept lashes, suddenly, gloriously aware of her power. He loved her!

'Laurel!' He said her name roughly, a warning and a plea, and she was the one who moved this time, curling herself into his arms, her fingers wantonly unfastening the buttons on his shirt, her palm flat against the racing urgency of his heart.

'All right, perhaps it is only physical,' he muttered thickly, 'but it could be the basis for something more, something. . . .'

He broke off, sweat moistening his skin, and her heart contracted in wonder and love.

'Oliver, it isn't just physical,' she told him shakily. 'I do love you. That's why I ran away. I thought you were just using me, and I couldn't stay.'

'Oh no!' he groaned hoarsely. 'So much wasted time! At first I did simply want to help you—or so I told myself. Try to understand, Laurel. All these years I've carried an immense burden of guilt about what I did. I tried to find you before, unsuccessfully, and then when we did meet and I found you so obviously emotionally scarred and so full of hate for me, I felt I had to try and reach you. But it was a plan that soon backfired on me. Perhaps now is the time to admit that that very first time we met you stirred something in me, something I had no right to feel, and because of that, crazily, I was harder on you than I might otherwise have been. My mother warned me I was being biased, but I wouldn't listen. I ought to explain that I was very close to Peter, my cousin, and his death. . . .' He broke off, and Laurel touched his hand compassionately.

'I'm just trying to excuse the inexcusable,' Oliver continued wryly, 'but at the time my emotions were so crazily mixed up. After Peter first died I dreamed continually about him, wondering if there wasn't some way I could save him, and somehow you became involved in that crusade. Realising the truth brought me to my senses, but by then it was too late, and my nightmares of Peter were replaced by nightmares of you, of your haunting, hurting expression!'

So that was why he had said she wasn't the only one to suffer from them!

'We met again, and this time I was determined to make atonement, but all the time I was at war with myself. One part of me wanted to be altruistic, to free you completely from the past, the other, jealous and possessive, wanted to free you so that you would turn to me—not any other man, just me, and I was fighting a constant battle against my love for you, fighting not to burden you with my feelings. I told myself I owed it to you to stand aside and let you make your own choices, but all the time . . . all the time I wanted you for myself,' he told her huskily. 'I wanted you to respond to me and only me, to love me as I realised I loved you. I told myself that it was unfair to you to try and trap you in a relationship with me purely on the basis that you responded to me physically, before you'd discovered more about life and love for yourself. But that didn't stop me from being jealous as hell when I thought you'd spent that night with Chas, giving him what you wouldn't give me. Then I was nearly demented with jealousy; just as I was tormented with my aching need for you every time I came anywhere near you. Sometimes I had to physically stop myself touching you. But I couldn't stop myself loving you. I thought I was destined to remain always confused in your mind with your stepfather.

'I used to dream about you,' Laurel admitted shakily. 'I used to dream it was you touching me and not him, and . . .' she took a deep breath,

confessing for the first time, 'and ... and in my
dream I liked having you touch me. Can't you
understand?' she pleaded with him. 'I had to bury
that even from myself because it was as though I
was admitting to myself that Bill Trenchard had
been right and I did want him. I told myself I
wanted to be revenged upon you, but. . . .'

Her words were silenced by the tender possession
of his mouth.

'Laurel.' When he released her she was still
quivering with the pleasure of his touch.

'I would never have gone with Chas, if I hadn't
read those notes, that book. . . .'

'What notes?'

Briefly she explained about the notes she had
seen when she went to get his jacket, and his frown
disappeared.

'Laurel, I wasn't making them because I
intended to write about you.' He cupped her face.
'As it happens, you are in my new book, we both
are, but not in the way you imagine. It's our story,
and I hope when you read it you'll agree with me
that it's the best thing I've ever done, but those
notes ... call it force of habit if you like, but they
were made simply to clarify my own thoughts. I
knew by then that it wasn't simply guilt that
motivated me, that my responses to you were far
from altruistic, and I was simply hoping that by
writing down what had happened in its purest
form I might be able to understand my own
emotions more. The notes merely confirmed what
I already knew in my heart—that I was hopelessly,
terrifyingly in love with you. As for the books,' he
grimaced faintly, 'I needed some books for
research into the subject of my next novel—while
we were in Provence an idea came to me for my
next book. When I worked as a reporter I did

some articles on long-stay prisoners and I wanted to do some investigations into the criminal personality—if indeed there is such a thing. I saw the other book while I was buying them and got it on impulse. By that time I was so crazily and desperately in love with you that I couldn't think straight any longer, and I thought that reading it might help me to understand and reach you. You see,' he said softly, 'we both leapt to the wrong conclusion; accused one another unfairly. When I saw what you'd written . . .! If you only knew you had a far more potent weapon at hand,' he told her, reminding her that he had used similar words then too. 'My love for you. . . .' he whispered against her ear.

'Can you forgive me?' he asked huskily, and there was a shadowing of pain in his eyes that told Laurel he would never entirely forgive himself for his original error of judgment. Her love for him welled up inside her, drowning out the past and all its pain.

'Only if you promise to forgive yourself,' she told him softly. 'To err is human, remember? And after what happened to Peter I can understand how in your bitterness. . . .'

'No,' he interrupted roughly, 'don't make excuses for me, Laurel. I can't think what I've ever done to deserve you,' he added throatily, brushing her skin with his lips. 'I want you to read my book. I wrote it for you,' he told her. 'A testimony of my love. It's more about me than you; about what I did to you; about the anguish of discovering my love. . . .'

Laurel put her finger against his lips, impelled to banish the bitter remorse in his eyes.

'Does it have a happy ending?'

For a moment Oliver looked nonplussed, and

then he saw her smile, and once more he was the urbane man she had first known.

'I'm more interested in happy beginnings,' he said slowly, responding to her mood, 'and I'm aching to get started on one right now. How quickly do you suppose we can be married? I doubt if Elizabeth will let us off with anything less than the whole thing, especially after all the trouble she's gone to to get you here.'

'She kept asking me if I thought you might love me,' Laurel told him happily.

'Umm, knowing all the time that I did ... although I suspect that even my sturdy sister would be surprised to learn that when I first felt the stirrings of that love you were barely fifteen. She kept on insisting that you weren't entirely indifferent to me, but I wanted to hear it from you, not her. Do you, Laurel?' he murmured seductively against her throat, his voice suddenly raw with a need that shivered across her nerves. 'Do you feel something for me?'

'Everything,' she assured him huskily, her blood singing with pleasure as he took her mouth, making his possession a statement and a pledge.

'Just as soon as I can I'm taking you to Provence,' he told her, reluctantly releasing her mouth, his hand sliding beneath her robe, cupping the rounded warmth of her breasts. 'This time as my wife, this time sharing my bed.'

Laurel looked up at him, her eyes demure, her body sending out a different more seductive message as she slid her arms round his neck.

'Soon?' she suggested hopefully, tugging his head down so that she could kiss him, her soft, 'very soon', lost against his lips as they parted hers insistently, re-affirming his love. Their love, she thought, in a daze of pleasure. A love she had never dreamed could be hers. She murmured a small sigh of pleasure and felt Oliver's arms tighten possessively round her.

'Very soon,' he promised huskily. 'The sooner the better!'

Harlequin® Plus

A WORD ABOUT THE AUTHOR

Born in Preston, a small city north of Liverpool, England, Penny Jordan was constantly in trouble as a schoolgirl because of her inability to stop daydreaming—the first sign of possible talent as a writer! When she was not daydreaming, she spent most of her spare time curled up somewhere with a book. Early in her teens she was introduced to romance novels and became an avid reader, but at the time it didn't occur to her to try to write one herself.

That changed when she entered her thirties and felt an urge to make a mark in the world by means of her own talent. She had many false starts—lots of "great" ideas ended up in the wastepaper basket. But finally the day came when Penny completed her first book-length manuscript. And, to her utter amazement, it wasn't long before the novel was accepted for publication.

Now she has received many letters of acceptance for her books, and every letter brings the thrill of knowing that the stories on which she has worked so hard will reach the readers for whom each is lovingly written.